SCARRED

Joanne Macgregor

OTHER YOUNG ADULT BOOKS BY THIS AUTHOR

Recoil (2016)
Refuse (2016)
Fault Lines (2016, Protea)
Rock Steady (2013, Protea)
Turtle Walk (2011, Protea)

If you would like to receive my author's newsletter, with tips on great books, a behind-the-scenes look at my writing and publishing processes, and advance notice of new books, giveaways and special offers, then sign up at my website, www.joannemacgregor.com.

First published in 2015 by KDP

Copyright 2015 Joanne Macgregor
The right of Joanne Macgregor to be identified as the author of this work has been asserted by her in accordance with sections 77 and 78 of the Copyright, Designs and Patents Act, 1988.

ISBN: 978-0-620-67859-9

ISBN: 978-0-620-67865-0 (epub)

For Emily,
my inspiration, my first reader, my biggest fan.

"To be alive at all is to have scars."
John Steinbeck

1

Full Frontal

Question: Can I do this? Answer: Do I have a choice?

I'm not sure I can do this, but I am sure that I can't carry on not doing it.

I am dead sick of hiding out like some wanted criminal, so I guess that means it's time to face the world. It's been nine months since someone pressed ctrl-alt-delete on my life, and it's time to reboot.

Today is Monday the fourteenth of August, the first day of the new school year. Today my life needs to change. Again.

This morning I will start my senior year at West Lake High – a different high school, in an old red brick building, right on the other side of town. I just couldn't face going back to my old school – the old classrooms, the old faces. That time now belongs to another person, to another life.

Today people can see me as I am and they, and I, will just have to deal with it. So I put down the foundation and sponge, take a last look in the mirror and grab my bag.

"Wish me luck," I say to the framed photograph of my mother perched on the living room shelf. (There is not, and never has been, a dad photo.)

Then I head for the door, pausing to snatch the newspaper article from the printer tray.

American Student in Africa mauled by chimp … loses ear, eye and parts of face.

Worse, yes, that was definitely worse. At least I still have my facial bits and pieces.

I stick this report – the latest in my collection of encouragingly bad news articles which have overflowed the confines of my corkboard and now trail in a steady line along the wall to the door – next to the piece with the headline, *Toddler, 3, sustains third degree burns to 80% of body and face.*

I *can* do this.

I am still telling myself this an hour later as I walk down the school hallway that leads from the administrative offices to the classroom to which I am headed, clutching my registration papers in my hand. I keep my chin up high, my hair tucked back behind my ears, my face on show for everyone to see. A few gazes linger a moment, then flick away, but mostly people just smile and nod in a friendly way and I smile back, full of determination and confidence, knowing to my bones that I can do this, and that *I. Am. Beautiful!*

Okay, so that's not what really happens. The bell for the first period has already rung and the hallways are mostly deserted as I scuttle along to room 33, clutching my registration papers in my sweaty hands. I keep my eyes on the floor and my head down so that my long hair swings in front of my face.

The classroom is on the ground floor. The door is already closed. I pause, flick my hair back over my shoulders and take a deep breath, then I push the handle down with my elbow and stride inside. This time my head is held high and I look straight at the teacher as I hand him the paperwork. I can do this part easily, because the left side of my face is all the kids behind the desks in the room can see. I'm aware of them, the scuffling and chatting and scraping of chairs, but I don't turn to face them. Not yet.

Oh, get a grip! And get on with it already.

Aloud, I say, "Mr. Perkel?"

The teacher looks like a wannabe intellectual refugee from some hipster university. He has thinning hair, a neatly clipped goatee beard, round John Lennon type spectacles, and he wears a worn, corduroy jacket with leather patches at the elbows.

"Aah," he says, quickly looking away from my face and staring down at the registration form like it's the one sheet of paper that might save humankind.

"We have a new student starting with us today."

I tilt my head slightly and look sideways at the class with my left eye. I take in many things at a glance. One wall of the classroom consists mostly of big windows which open onto grassy lawns just outside. Curl-cornered posters of Byron, Shakespeare, Emily Dickinson and Mark Twain are stuck on the back wall, and the floor is red and green checkered linoleum. There are about twenty students in the room, and all of them are turning to look at me. But my eyes have snapped to just one face.

It's him! Luke Naughton – from swimming meets, from before. All caramel hair and hazel eyes in the middle of the second row. And he sees me, recognizes me. Time stretches out slowly and sweetly like a piece of soft toffee. I can feel a smile beginning to curl my lips, see one sneaking up lopsidedly onto his, when Mr. Perkel introduces me.

"This is –" he checks the paper again, and my moment to go full-frontal has arrived. I turn to face *him*, the class and the world as Mr. Perkel says, "Sloane Munster".

All eyes flick to my right cheek – I know it, I can feel my response in the heat rising up from my neck – but I see only him. His eyes move to my scar. He actually turns his head to take it in, the smile stillborn on his face. His lips twist, but in a sneer, not a smile. Then he looks back into my eyes and this time his are full of deep revulsion.

2

Exposed

It's like a kick in the gut, that look from Luke. What the hell ...?

Mr. Perkel stuffs books and notes into my hands and urges me to take a seat. Desperate to turn my back on Luke's angry look, I fling myself into the first empty chair I see – behind the first desk in the row alongside the windows which overlook the football fields. This is a mistake. Now the right side of my face is exposed for the whole class to see. Good. Let them look their fill and get it over with. I can hear a few whispers and snickers and "OMG's" from behind me, but I ignore these – they were only to be expected. What gets to me is *his* look. I can still feel it now, burning into me like a laser from where he sits, behind and to the right of me.

In an attempt to convince myself that I'm being paranoid, that I imagined his expression, I turn to glance quickly over my shoulder. He's still doing it – glaring at me – his eyes livid and repelled and condemning. What *is* his problem? He's looking at me like a monk would look at a naked drunk vomiting in the street. Like I'm something obscene.

Well, this is a first.

I'm used to blank looks of shock, quick winces of pity, curious stares and careful avoidance of same. But never has someone scowled at me as if I did something wrong, like I voluntarily acquired my disfigurement to ruin their view. I sneak another glance and this time he's actually shaking his head as if in disgust at me.

I'm hurt, there's no denying it. But I would rather eat sloth spit than show him that. So I take comfort in anger, in mentally abusing the kind of pig who shows his repulsion and aversion to disfigurement – shows it clearly and honestly to the disfigured person in question, no less, rather than sniggering over it with his buddies in private. The rules of civilized society say we must conceal our automatic reactions of disgust. It might be natural to respond with repugnance, but we're supposed to hide this under a nice false veneer of polite indifference. He, obviously, is too stupid to master the rules of social pretense and insincerity. Moron.

I resolve to ignore him – after first shooting back a glare of my own – and spend the rest of the lesson alternating between listening to snatches of Mr. Perkel and making strategic plans to find, in future, seats on the other side of the classroom and preferably toward the back, so as to minimize facial exposure. This doesn't count as a retreat into the concealment closet. Just because I've stopped hiding doesn't mean I have to be on full display.

When the bell rings, I let the rest of the class leave the room first. When Luke passes my desk, stepping deliberately and carefully over my bag as if the touch of it on his toe might contaminate him, I can feel the sneer. I hold myself still, unbreathing – like a small critter playing possum until the predator passes, my face hidden in my hair.

3

Eyes

I have red hair. It's a true dark red, not orange, so I don't get called carrot-top or ginger or worse, orangutan – which is what some kids called an orange-haired girl at my old school. I didn't used to get called anything nasty about my appearance, I used to be pretty. *The GG's* – short for Gorgeous Girls – that's what our clique of girls was called, in my old school. We gave ourselves the name. It makes me cringe to think of it now. Who was that girl that looked like me, but behaved so obnoxiously?

I still have the oval face, the milk-pale skin with only a few freckles over the bridge of my nose which turns up slightly at the end – it's called *retroussé,* according to Mom – and the blue eyes. But it's not these things that anyone notices, not anymore. All anyone sees now, all I see now, is the scar which stretches in a red diagonal slash across my right cheek from just below the outer corner of my eye, to the edge of my upper lip.

I know that it could be a lot worse. The scar is not puckered and it doesn't have a thick, raised ridge. At the hospital they told me that they got a plastic surgeon to stitch it up and they say he did a great job, but plastic surgery can't fix all scars and mine is here to stay. The doc told me that, in time, it would probably fade to a whitish-silver line. I read up all about scars on the internet. Turns out that "in time" means "in a few years", and "probably" means "maybe". In the meantime, I'm stuck with it.

It ends in a little sickle, as if it was a hook just slightly lifting up the edge of my mouth. I worry that it makes me look as if I'm sneering at everything. My shrink, Eileen, says it makes me look as if I'm smiling at life. She says that I am still beautiful. Ha, no chance of that. You can tell by my eyes that I'm definitely not smiling, and anyone can see that I'm no beauty.

My shrink also said I had to "take back my eyes". (She has said a lot of things; some of them have stuck.)

"You've stopped seeing," she said. "You've stopped looking at anything or anyone else. It's like your eyes have rolled back inwards and all you can see is yourself and that scar. You've reduced yourself to a three inch red line!"

"It's actually closer to four inches."

Shrinks aren't supposed to let their emotions show, but I guess she was pretty frustrated with me by then, because her ears went red and she banged the palm of her hand on the arm of her chair.

"It's ridiculous! Take back your eyes and look around you at the world. Look at a sunset, watch ants walking in a line on the sidewalk, look at other people – and *not* just to see how they notice and react to your face!"

"Okay, okay! I'll try."

"Either do or do not – there is no try!" she said in a Yoda voice which made me smile – a real smile, not my scar-smirk – but it disappeared with her next words.

"This week, I'm giving you homework."

"You get homework in therapy?" Figures.

"You do. Take some of that money you feel so guilty about having, and buy a nice new digital camera."

"My homework is to buy a camera?"

"Your homework is to take pictures. I'm *hoping*," she said "hoping", but from her expression it looked more like she was begging and pleading, perhaps even praying, "that it will force you to look outside of yourself. To look at other people, other things, and to stop focusing so obsessively on your own face. You're more focused on your appearance than a beauty queen – it's a kind of reverse vanity!"

That stung.

I did what she said. I bought the camera and I learned how to work it (no mean feat, given the number of buttons and settings), so now I take pictures and, actually, I quite enjoy it. I don't know that I'm any good, but I *can* confirm that a nice big camera, held with hands on either side, covers up most of the photographer's face. It also makes people self-conscious about themselves when you point a lens at them, and then they stop staring at you in a hurry.

At our last session, Eileen gave me more homework. And this assignment is going to be a lot tougher than clicking off a few pics. She got me, by dint of persuasion, arguments of logic, appeals to emotion, demands, pleas, and every other kind of therapeutic manipulation, to agree to come out of the camouflage closet. Today, when I started at my new school, I had to stop disguising my scar and show my whole face.

I have been in hiding – there's no denying that. Like a winter creature in hibernation, I have stayed close to my den of an apartment. My venturing out has mainly been online and inside. When I have *had* to brave the world, to go to my weekly therapy session or for a doctor's checkup, I've spent hours in front of the mirror on disguise detail.

I ordered this thick, skin-colored goop called *Derma Cover* from an online shopping site. Whenever I go out, I smear it over the scar and the rest of my face. From a few feet back, it looks okay, but there is no denying that up-close, it looks nasty-ass. Like I have a gross skin disease. So I have taken to putting it on not quite so thickly – there's no way to fill in the dent of the scar, anyway – and resorting to other disguises: giant J-Lo type sunglasses, carefully draped scarves, and hair styled to hang in a wave over my right cheek. I briefly toyed with the idea of getting one of those Groucho

Marx plastic moustache-nose-glasses disguises but, while it would hide my identity, it would do nothing to cover the scar.

"This camouflage is not necessary. You would care less what people thought of you if you knew how seldom they did," my shrink said. She says this often.

"They stare," I always reply.

"They're probably staring because you wear sunglasses inside, scarves in summer and keep your head permanently tilted to cover your face with hair like some Wookie!"

"People stare," I merely repeat, nestling my cheek in my hand to ease the crick in my neck which the head tilting has given me. Resting your cheek in your hand is also a good hiding trick, but I can confirm that it looks weird if you do it while walking or standing.

People *do* stare. I don't get angry at them – well, not anymore. I know they're just curious. I see how they try to avert their eyes immediately after the first shock and I know they mean no harm. Heck, I would probably stare, too – if the scar was on the other face. But it means I can never forget. I can never lose myself in a moment or an experience because their stares always remind me of what happened. I am tethered by the scar to that day, the day when everything changed.

The me I was then is gone. It's like an alien spaceship hovered over my life, sucked me up, transmogrified me and then spat me out into another existence. I'm different – inside and out. Those girls I used to hang out with, with their silly preoccupations and worries – I don't belong with them anymore. They came, some of them, to visit me in the hospital, but it was obvious they felt uncomfortable. They couldn't look me straight in the eye, couldn't see past the injuries and didn't know what to say. I didn't encourage them to return and when I told them I needed to be alone to heal, they didn't force the issue.

After I left the hospital and moved to my new apartment, I ignored their calls and allowed them to drift away. There were a few messages on my seventeenth birthday, but eventually the calls stopped.

I have become my scar. It is what people notice first and remember last about me. Out of embarrassment, or perhaps fear of embarrassing me, they look away quickly and whisper to their gawping children not to stare. They look around me, behind me, to the side of me – anywhere but directly at me. It is as if I am both glaringly obvious and completely invisible. Those who stick around beyond the first few seconds don't last much longer. They try – I can see them almost breaking out in a sweat with the effort of it – not to look at the red slash. But it pulls their eyes irresistibly, a magnet on iron filings, until they look, and then look again and then give up and move off to something or someone less exhausting, less riveting, less ugly.

But I have promised Eileen, and made a vow to myself, to start this school year differently. This is the trade-off for giving in to the temptation to run away from my old school and begin somewhere new instead.

And so here I am, at West Lake High, having my bare face stared at by a whole new set of faces and eyes.

Or, to be more accurate, having my bare face glared at by Luke.

4

Freaks

When Luke leaves the English classroom, air rushes back into my lungs and I can find enough of my voice to get directions to the next class – Art – from the teacher.

As I walk into the art room, I notice two things. One, *he's* not in this class. (Of course not – he's probably brushing up his skills in an advanced program rudeness tutorial.) And two, there's an empty desk about halfway up the row alongside the hallway wall, where the scarred side of my face would offend only the beige paint. I make a beeline for the seat while the teacher – a skinny woman who smells of cigarette smoke and peppermints and wears several layers of floaty clothes – introduces me to the class. This, according to my schedule, is Miss Ling.

"This is Sloane Munster," she announces, wasting no energy on smiles or enthusiasm.

"Sloane Monster, more like."

It's a whispered comment which comes from one of a group of girls I recognize from English class. There are four of them, fashionably dressed and carefully made-up, with perfect hair and unscarred faces, and they are clustered at the back of the room, riding their chairs. The wisecrack is met with a few smug giggles. The girls are reassured by my obvious disqualification from the beauty stakes.

"Hi." The girl seated in front of me has turned around and is smiling at me. "I'm Sienna."

She is tiny. She looks too small to be a senior. She has a heart-shaped faced, round brown eyes and a halo of corkscrew curls which bounce when she nods her chin in the direction of the girls.

"Don't mind them. They're a bunch of no-talents who only signed up for art class because they thought it would teach them how to apply their make-up better."

"Hi, Sienna. Sloane," I say, pointing a thumb at my chest.

Miss Ling calls the class to order and is about to close the door when a boy walks in. He takes up most of the doorway and when he sinks into a chair a few desks in front and to the left of me, he overflows. He's big. Not fat, exactly, but bulky and somehow out of proportion. His hair is cut very short around a face with a doughy pallor, and his head seems too small for the massive body beneath. He wears jeans, heavy Doc Marten boots and a red plaid shirt.

"I'm a lumberjack and I'm alright, I work all day and I sleep all night." The girls at the back sing the chorus softly.

"No singing in this class," says Miss Ling. To the boy, she says, "You're late."

He doesn't reply. He drops his bag on the desk with a thud that makes me jump. Loud noises still do that to me, as do the sounds of breaking glass and screeching brakes. But I am not going to allow the pressing memory into my mind right now.

The Shrink taught me that staring hard at an object is a useful way of staying grounded in the present, so right now I focus on the big boy's bag. It's a plain, gray, rectangular bag, with a single shoulder strap. A peace symbol, which looks like it's been wrought from barbed wire, has been sketched in black ink over the whole of the front flap. Written underneath the graphic, in rough lettering, is, "Give peace a chance".

Miss Ling walks between the desks, handing out sketch paper and chalky pastels in a range of earth colors. The big, dough-faced boy says nothing, merely looks down at the paper that is deposited onto the desk in front of him. He picks up a dark umber-colored pastel and draws a series of crossed lines over the back of one hand.

Miss Ling places a narrow earthenware vase on the table. It is filled with stalks of dried wheat and barley. She removes a few of the stalks and drops them carelessly alongside the base of the vase.

"I would like a sketch of this still-life by the end of this double lesson," she says. "Pay particular attention to shading and cross-hatching. And try to keep the noise down."

She sits behind her desk, plugs in the ear-buds of an iPod, and closes her eyes, resting her head against the back of the chair and putting her feet up on the desk.

"Laziest teacher ever," says Sienna. "But at least you can do what you like in her class. She doesn't ever actually teach, but she doesn't interfere either, and she always passes everyone."

I sketch a few lines of the vase and glance around the class to see what the others are doing. The girls at the back are drawing vases of flowers – childishly doodled roses and daisies which bear no resemblance to the vase of dried grasses. Sienna is right, they are not artistically gifted. To the left of me, a pale boy with dark hair and long sideburns quickly draws a tiny vase with cramped, narrow strokes in the bottom corner of his sheet, then he flips the paper over and rapidly doodles a series of big, bold Anime cartoons of the kids in the class. He gives me flowing straight red hair and oriental eyes, but I recognize myself from the slashed line across one cheek. The girls at the back of the class are all hair, teeth and boobs in his rendering.

The big boy's drawing looks nothing like Miss Ling's vase, but it shows real talent. He has made the vase angular – a series of jagged, spikey slanted lines like the broken-mirror pattern of lights that crosses my vision when I get a migraine. He has drawn the wheat and barley as articulated chains of nuts and bolts and nails.

"He's good," I say to Sienna, nodding at the mechanical graphic.

"Yeah, he's got skillz," she replies.

"Hey, El-Jayyyy," calls one of the girls from the back. "How's your drawing coming on? Wouldn't you rather be, like, chopping trees?"

This provokes giggles and a fresh round of the lumberjack song.

"What's his name?" I ask, speaking softly.

"L.J."

"How do you spell that?"

"Like the initials, L.J. Don't ask me what they stand for – because nobody knows and he's not telling. Even the teachers have called him that ever since he started high school here."

"We call him Lumber-Jack," says a busty blonde girl from the back. She makes no effort to keep her voice down.

"Why?"

The girl looks at me like I'm stupid. "Have you seen how he walks?"

I get it then. He lumbers. The red plaid shirt doesn't help either, I guess, if he's not trying to look like a frontiersman. Apparently, I am not the only freak in this school. I wonder if Luke glares at this boy, too. I look back at L.J. His wide shoulders ripple and twitch as if he is trying to dislodge an irritating fly, but otherwise he does not respond to the taunts from the back of the class.

Sienna's sketch is coming on well, but she is dissatisfied.

"I'm not that good at drawing and painting, if you want the truth. Photography's my thing. I know a good picture when I see it, and it's easier to capture it in pixels than pastels."

"I just got a digital camera," I say, smudging the shading on my vase with the tip of a finger. "I'm having fun with it, but I don't really think I know what I'm doing. It's hella complicated."

"I can give you a few tips, if you like," volunteers Sienna.

"That would be great."

"There's also a photography club here at the school – maybe you'd like to join that? It meets on Friday nights at the Pizza place down the road. They're a nice crowd. You'd like them."

I hesitate. I've avoided clubs and groups since … well, for most of the last year. I don't know that I'm brave enough yet to plunge back into a full social life.

"Are you a member?"

"Nah, it's a bit basic for me. Sorry – that sounds really arrogant – it's just that I've been doing this for years, and the club is more for people just starting out." Sienna grabs my paper and holds it up to admire the sketch. "Hey, you're good, too."

"It's okay," It's no Van Gogh, but at least my wheat stalks don't look like kindergarten daisies. "So do you do the photography for something in particular, or just for fun?" I ask Sienna.

"I have an online blog – it's called *Underground West Lake*. The school has this really boring e-newsletter here, called the West Lake News. It's a weekly newsletter, but it's written mainly by the staff and it's just sports events and results, and rah-rah pep-talks about building character in difficult times, and don't forget to bring canned soup for the next charity drive. Riveting stuff like that. So I started the blog. It's supposed to be subversive, but it's mostly a lot of gossip, and some humor. Keith here –" she gestures to the boy drawing the Anime cartoons and he waves an absent greeting at me, "does cartoon panels for us. We have '10 best and worst' lists, and it's linked to a twitter feed. I'm the web-mistress-slash-editor, but I also do a lot of pics, photographic essays, sneak-shots – just to give a feel of life at the school, you know?"

"It sounds amazing!"

I am impressed. How does anyone have that much energy? It takes everything I have just to get through each day.

"I think it's pretty cool, if I do say so myself." Sienna grins. "You should go online and check it out. *www.undergroundwestlake.com*. Let me know if there's anything you can contribute – an article or maybe some photos. You could bring a fresh perspective. You know, a noob's view of this place."

"Maybe," I say.

So far, my day confirms my belief that this place is pretty much like any place. This could be Somewhere High, Anywheresville. There are the usual mix of people: nice, nasty, pretentious, humble, lazy, talented and weird. There's only one unpleasantly abnormal person here. And it's not L.J. Or me.

The rest of the day passes quickly in a confusion of various rooms, different teachers, crowded halls and new classmates. Today, Luke was only in my English and Math classes, but I haven't had all my subjects yet. Tomorrow I'll find out if he's in any of the others. It's a possibility that makes my stomach clench.

Back at home, I take my vitamins, check my temperature – normal – and then go online. I have a Facebook page on which I never post. I use it to spy on others – it makes a nice change from having everyone stare at me. It takes me a minute or two, but I find Luke's page. At least, I think it's his. The profile picture is of a hand reaching out above the blue, rippled surface of a pool, but the face and body are under the water. I click on *timeline*, *about*, *photos*, but strike out. His security must be set to maximum, and I don't dare send a friend request.

Then I remember *Sink-or-Swim*, the website that we all used to hang out on, when I was still swimming competitively. I haven't been on it for ages, not since the day I got the scar, so it takes a few tries to get my username and password right. Then I'm in and staring at his profile. His handle is *Not_A*. Not a ... what? It was one of the things I wanted to ask him before, but I never got the chance. The photo is a close-up of him staring seriously into the camera. I think it's different to the one he used to have up. He used to be smiling in his profile pic, I'm sure of it. And there's a way I can check.

At the bottom of the hall closet, under a jumble of flippers, kickboards, hand paddles and swimming caps, is a large cardboard box, covered with doodles and stickers. I called it my memory box and used to keep little mementos like concert ticket stubs, birthday cards, and notes from friends safely inside. That was when I still had memories I wanted keep. These days, I'd like to have a memory trashcan.

I open the box and just below a couple of photographs of old friends, I find what I'm looking for. The printed swim meet program is puckered and smudged where water once dripped on it – I only kept it because his hand had touched it. Underneath it is my old cellphone, the one with photos taken at meets, and screenshots of his profile on the swimming website. Predictably, its battery is totally dead, so I plug it in to charge, and go back to examining every detail about Luke I can find online.

Under his profile pic on *Sink-or-Swim* is the briefest of bio's: "Swimmer, son, survivor, cynic". There's a feature where you list your favorites. His favorite song: *Pompei* by Bastille (I've never heard of it); his favorite movie: *Inception*; food: Mexican; animals: puppies (aww!). Under *personal motto*, he has, "Vivere commune est, sed non commune mereri". I look it up on Google. It means, "Everybody lives; not everybody deserves to". Okkaayyy, then.

I check his swimming times in the meets for the past year. Seems like he had a slump for a while there, but his times are improving steadily. Then I click through to the forums, but I can't find any comments from him on any recent topics. In the archived section, I find an old thread that makes me smile.

Not_A:	Great race today!
WaterBaby:	You were watching? O_0
Not_A:	Watching you? Sure!
WaterBaby:	:)
Not_A:	Saw you win the 100m Butterfly – nice one! Personal best time?
WaterBaby:	Yeah, but didn't break the record. L
Not_A:	Yet ...
WaterBaby:	:D
Not_A:	Gotta go. Mom's calling dinner-time, and she freaks out if we're late to the table. See you at the meet on the 17th?
WaterBaby:	Definitely.
Not_A:	D: D:
Not_A:	Bye (Water)baby.
WaterBaby:	See you later.

I sigh and check the phone, but the battery's only at 2%. Perhaps Luke is on Twitter. I sign on, seek and find. His handle is @LukeSkyWater, the bio is the same as on *Sink-or-Swim*, the photo the same as from

Facebook. It's a puzzling picture. Is it the hand of someone waving, or drowning?

I scan his tweet-stream. It seems he doesn't tweet often, but there's one from today:

That moment when you can't believe what you're seeing. #Disgusted #Angry

Have I just been sub-tweeted? Is he talking about me?

This is ridiculous. To distract myself, I close the social sites and check out Sienna's alternative school blog. It's hilarious. I wish my mom was here tonight to see it. It's exactly her kind of thing – clever and witty and edgy. There was nothing like this at my previous school.

Memories threaten, but I push them back and down, breathe deeply three times and force myself to concentrate on the screen in front of me. There are sketched caricatures of the teachers, Keith's Anime cartoons (the one of me in art class is already up), informal news articles and a gallery of photographs of students, teachers and scenes of school life. I examine these carefully. It's several minutes before I realize that what I'm actually doing is searching for a picture of Luke. I realize I've been cyber-stalking him all evening.

Clearly, I'm an idiot. My scars, apparently, are the least of my defects.

The view from the other side

Luke

She's here. Here! At West Lake High. In my English class.

Same ruby red hair, freckles and big blue eyes as that last day I saw her, when I almost learned her name. Well, I sure know it now: Sloane Munster.

What I don't know, is what she's doing here. Did she know I was at West Lake? Is that why she came? Does she want something from me?

I could tell she recognized me immediately.

She doesn't look exactly the same as she used to, though. She's taller and thinner, and there's a look in her eyes like she expects to be kicked. And of course there's that scar everyone's talking about.

That scar!

I don't even know how to look at her.

6

Back in the water

It's day two of my life out of the camouflage closet and I get my driver, Ed, to take me to school early. Ed is fiftyish and friendly, an all-round good guy, and he gets well-paid by the trust to take me wherever I need to go. But he nags me too often about when I intend to learn how to drive myself, even volunteers to teach me. I tell him he's crazy – if I learn to drive then he'll be out of a job. I tell him that he's lucky I'm too lazy to learn how to drive. I'm not sure he buys it.

I need to start the things I have resolved to do, before I lose my nerve. And so, today, I have to get back into the swim of things. West Lake High has its own pool – one of the reasons I chose this school – big and deep and, thankfully, heated. At this hour of the morning, as I hoped, it's also empty. I slip off my sweats, put on my cap and goggles, and dive into the still water. My every splash sounds loudly in the cathedral-like silence. Steam rises off the water, condenses on the insulated roof above and falls back in cold drops onto my face as I swim my twenty lengths of backstroke. It's good to be back in the water. My arms and legs cleave cleanly through the silky softness, the water hides my face, my goggles fog up, insulating me further from the world beyond my cocoon of movement, and my mind is focused only on the next stroke, the next breath, the next length.

I've done my breast-stroke and am deeply in the zone of my freestyle set when there's an explosion of bubbles and shifting water next to me. In surprise, I breathe in some water through my nose and stop, mid-stroke, coughing and looking around. What must be the entire swim team has arrived for morning training. They are noisily snapping towels at each other and dive-bombing into the water. It's my cue to leave.

I swim to the side, lift the goggles off my eyes and onto my head and, still coughing, pull myself awkwardly out of the water. Sometimes, like now, my knee sticks and won't bend properly. I'm like a stranded water creature, clumsily hauling myself onto the brick surround and then scrambling awkwardly to my feet. As I stand, dripping, my eyes follow up the muscled legs, green towel, toned midriff and wide shoulders of the boy who stands in front of me, blocking my way. It's him, of course, captain of the swim team and sneerer-in-chief. He looks like he looked a year ago, beside a different pool, but he also looks – I don't know – *more*. I look away from his curled lips and harsh eyes, focus instead on his ripped abs and muscled arms. This is not too much of a hardship and I could probably stand there, dripping wet and feasting my eyes all day, but my gaze is drawn back up to his and a ball of hurt knots tightly in my stomach. His eyes seem more gold than green today, and there is no relenting softness in his look.

"Um, excuse me?" I try to step around him. I'm cooling down rapidly and my skin is tightening all over with goose bumps. I cross my arms over my chest.

"So you still swim?" he asks, making no move to get out of my way.

"Yes." This confirms it – he does recognize me from before. "Just for fun, I mean. I don't race anymore. I ..."

My voice trails off under his withering glare. It irks me that I have to look up to meet his gaze. Normally it's a novelty when a guy is taller than me, but right now it would be great to be able to look down on him – literally.

"How nice for you," he says, and his voice sounds bitter. "That you can still have *fun*." He makes it sound like a dirty word.

"Look –" I begin, annoyed and determined to challenge him on his rude and inexplicable attitude.

"You have a real *fun* day, now," he says, ripping the towel off from around his waist.

I flinch and step back, half expecting him to lash out at me with it, but he just flings it aside and steps past me to dive into the pool, his body cutting through the water with hardly a splash.

I release the breath that I've been holding onto as if it was my last, and watch him for a few moments, torn between relief, confusion and growing anger, before I head for the changing rooms. I have both English and Math today. Maybe I'll have a chance to confront him and ask him what his problem is then.

7

Working pairs

The first class of the day – History – is mercifully a Luke-free zone and I happily sit with Sienna. Afterwards, she heads off to Spanish and I'm stuck in a double-period of something called Life Orientation. It's a stupid subject meant to teach us skills to cope with life. We had something similar at my previous school. Everyone finds it boring, no-one takes it seriously, but we all have to do the work because the grades count. Today, it goes so horribly wrong, it may as well be called Life Disorientation.

First off, His Royal Rudeness is most definitely in this class. He alternates scowling grimly at me with ignoring me completely. Secondly, the hair-teeth-boobs girls are in this class, too, sitting in a group right in front of me. I would have chosen another seat, but this is the only one where I'm behind and out of Luke's direct line of sight. It's an important tactical advantage, but it doesn't stop the death-stares. The girls alternate between flirting with Luke – he is clearly hot property – and coming up with new nicknames for me. They smile and laugh while they do it, so the teacher probably assumes they are being friendly. A dark girl with fine, doll-like features is still rooting for "Scar Monster".

"We could call her Monster for short. Or just Scar – like in Lion King," she sniggers.

But the leader of the pack, a blonde-haired, tan-skinned, brown-eyed beauty whose name, if I heard correctly, is Juliet, has a different suggestion.

"How about 'Scarface'?" she says softly, and looks over her shoulder at me to see my reaction, smiling like a shark before the bite.

It's genius. And hilarious. I tell them so.

"Those are really clever names," I say, deadpan. "Original. And side-splittingly funny. You should go into stand-up comedy, definitely."

They look momentarily confused, but then Juliet whispers something into their midst and they erupt in giggles. Despite my outward cool, my inner furnace must be turned to maximum, because I can feel my face glowing red. The scar feels like it is actually throbbing, though I must be imagining this.

This classroom is located in the center of the school, and has no windows. The back wall is a collage of beautiful photographs – beach sunsets, misty mountains, full moons over desert dunes, perhaps originally from some large calendar – studded with inspirational words: *reach, inspire, forgive, love, dream.*

Gag. The side walls are more prosaically decorated with posters urging us to shun the multiple evils of drugs, alcohol, bullying, teenage pregnancy, distracted driving and unsafe sex.

The teacher claps her hands together, calling the class to order. Her name is Mrs. Copeman, but no doubt the girls have another name for her, too. Her dumpy figure and flat, sensible shoes would invite their scorn. I think I'm going to like her – she has a friendly, open face and smiles often as she introduces the new theme.

"This term, we'll be focusing on pollution." She ignores the groans and disparaging comments from the students. "And you'll be doing a two-part practical project" – more complaints – "for which you'll be working in pairs."

There are squeals from the group of girls at this and they clutch at each other, partnering up already, although from under her thickly mascaraed lashes, Juliet casts a speculative look at Luke. This makes a change from her usual, faintly surprised expression because although her eyes are a pretty chestnut brown, they do protrude just the slightest bit.

"For the first part of the project, each pair will be assigned a type of pollution that affects our different senses. For example, our sense of sight is affected by visual pollution such as litter and graffiti. Our sense of sound gets hammered with noise pollution from noisy trucks and aircraft, and the jackhammers of road workers. Our taste buds, and our bodies in general, are polluted by food additives and chemicals, and our sense of smell is polluted by smoke, diesel fumes, the smell coming off landfills, and the like. I've left out the sense of touch, because it was quite hard coming up with examples, but if anyone wants to do it, just come chat with me. You'll need to do a theory section which describes your type of pollution, gives examples, and looks at methods of remediation and prevention. Plus I want a practical section with examples of the pollution – photographs, or sound recordings, or whiffs which I could sniff."

"Yeah, we could do, like, a scratch 'n sniff of your armpit, Doug," says Juliet.

"Or a sound-bite of your voice," comes the snappy reply. I laugh, and Juliet turns to give me a filthy look.

"How would you capture an example of taste pollution?" someone asks.

"Perhaps you could include a sample of the item to be tasted, along with a label of the ingredients," Mrs. Copeman suggests while handing out typed instruction sheets. "Here is the assignment description and rubric. Right, now for the working pairs."

Around her, people are already choosing partners. I sit still, in a puddle of embarrassed dread. I don't know anyone in the class – at least, no-one who would want to work with me.

"Don't get carried away. I'll be assigning partners alphabetically. It's important," Mrs. Copeman has to raise her voice over the protests, "that you are able to work with different people. Learning how to stay flexible and adjust to change is part of what Life Orientation is about."

She picks up a class-list and starts pairing off students. Juliet is a Capstan, not a Capulet, though it's close enough to give me the giggles when her name is read out. She gives me more of the stink-eye and tosses a lock of golden hair over her shoulder as she walks over to sit alongside a geeky boy called Tyrone Carter. He swallows several times and looks like he can't believe his luck.

For some reason, more surnames seem to begin with an M than with any other letter, but Munster is the last.

The third bad thing in this class – and it's the worst thing, definitely – happens when I get paired with the first N – Naughton. Luke Naughton.

How can this be happening? Really, what are the odds?

Luke sighs deeply and turns to face me. He obviously hates the idea of having me for a partner. All those close-up views of my face will no doubt put him off his lunch. He asks Mrs. Copeman if we can change partners.

"No, Luke. I just told you that part of this project is learning to work with new partners and I'm sure Sloane will be more than up to the demands of this task. Now, one person from each pair needs to come up here and stick a paw in this bag to choose a pollution type."

Luke slumps in his chair, making no move to come to my desk or to approach Mrs. Copeman. After a few minutes, I get up, stick my hand in the bag she is holding and pull out a slip of paper. Then I sit down in the chair Juliet vacated, in the row next to Luke.

"We have to do visual pollution," I say.

No response.

"Pollution that affects our sense of sight."

"I get it," he says flatly.

He turns to me, stony-faced. His eyes are a deep green, ringed by a border of golden-brown. The look in them is unreadable but, still, they accomplish their usual trick of sucking the air out of my lungs. An awkward silence burgeons between us. I force myself to take a slow, steadying breath.

"Um, look, I can see the idea of us working together thrills you about as much as it does me. How about we divide up the work and then each do our sections as separately as possible?"

"Fine."

"Would you prefer to do —"

"Whatever," he snaps.

"Okay ..."

I clear my throat – something is making it hard to swallow – and turn to the printed page of instructions. I'm trying to stay cool, to act like his behavior doesn't affect me, but my traitor eyes are prickling hotly. I clench a hand, digging my fingernails into my palm in painful distraction. I will not cry – not here, not now, and never in front of him.

"I have a camera, so I could do the pictures of pollution if you're okay with doing the theory section."

"Fine."

I consult my schedule and see that we have L.O. only once a week, in this slot.

"So maybe we should make a first pass at our sections and bring them next week?" I suggest.

"Email," he says, passing me his instruction sheet. I take it by the other end, careful not to let my fingers touch his.

"Huh?"

"What's your email address?" He enunciates each word carefully, as if I'm a mental incompetent.

"Oh, right."

I scrawl it on the sheet, and hand it back. He obviously wants to keep me at internet-distance, whenever possible. He doesn't volunteer his email address, and I'll be damned if I ask him.

There is nothing more to say. All around us, the other students are chatting away – some about the assignment, some about their plans for Labor Day weekend. Tyrone Carter is in a geek-spasm – treating Juliet to a long lecture about how corrupted files and computer viruses can destroy a PC's hard-drive and should be considered "information pollution". Alone in the class, Luke and I sit in silence. I jot down some ideas for places where I could take pictures of pollution, and write a reminder to buy a bigger memory card for my camera and some photographic paper for my printer. He plays with a pen, circling it between his long fingers and occasionally tapping it on the pad of paper in front of him. His every movement speaks of deep irritation.

Neither of us says another word or looks at the other until the bell for the lunch-break rings. I'm brown-bagging it today – I have given myself permission not to have to eat in the crowded cafeteria – and I long to escape to the shade under the large oak which grows on the slope bordering the fields outside. Automatically, I take a pack of anti-bacterial wipes out of my bag, remove one, and clean my hands.

Luke stares at the wipe, then gives me a brief, disbelieving look before slinging his bag over one shoulder and heading out. I crumple the square of white and drop it in the bin. My appetite is gone.

8

Focus

Luke

A class full of potential partners, and I get paired with Sloane Munster. It's like I can't get away from this. Or her.

I try to ignore her, but that's impossible. She's everywhere. In the pool when I want to swim, in my way in the halls, in my L.O. class as my project partner when I'd rather work with anyone else. In my head when I try to think of anything else.

It pisses me off. *She* pisses me off.

She says she'll go ask Copeman again to ask if we can change, but I know it won't help. It's not right, it's not fair. But I've learned that's just how the world works.

So she's all peppy about the project. Full of suggestions as to how we can do it. Doesn't she get it? At all?

She must. She does. From the way she tries to steer clear of me, I can tell she knows this is getting to me. She's wound pretty tight – as tight as mom – and all folded in on herself like a paper clip. She goes red when the girls get on her case, grips her things like they'll spin out away from her if she loosens her hold, and keeps trying to hide that damn scar. I'd feel sorry for her only, you know, I don't.

I need to stop thinking about her and focus on my times. This afternoon I'll just swing by to visit Moses for a few minutes and then I'll go on to evening practice. First dry land strength-training, then drills, then sprints. Coach wants me to break 1:55 on the 200m freestyle. He says he believes I can do it. Do I believe it? I'd better. I've got to lift my game unless I want to be stuck at home for ever.

And what's with her germ phobia? It's pathetic.

9

Not enamored

Question: Are things going well? Answer: Are they, hell!

It's day three of my new life. Before lunch, I have history and art (no problems) and then English (problems).

I shun the front-of-class seat I sat in on the first day and find one right in the back corner, along the wall that separates the classroom from the hallway. There's a row of small windows high up on the wall and the poster of Lord Byron broods directly over my seat. It's a good seat for hiding out in, and it will be warm in winter: there is a radiator alongside my desk, and a pipe leads from it up along the pillar of the wall between windows, and disappears into the ceiling.

I wish I could follow it.

I didn't notice it last time, but L.J. is also in this class. He lurks in a seat at the back, too, but whereas I am hiding from Luke, I think L.J. is trying to get as far away from Mr. Perkel as possible. I don't blame him. This teacher really seems to have it in for him.

Mr. Perkel, who is wearing a blue bowtie today, kicks off the lesson by giving the class a word of the day.

"Enamored," he sounds each syllable of the word distinctly as he writes it on the board. "From the Latin prefix *en* and the root *amor*. Can anyone tell me what it means?"

No-one volunteers.

"Mr. Hamel?" Perkel looks at L.J. with a raised eyebrow. L.J. shrugs, says nothing.

"Don't know? How unusual. I'm amazed," Perkel says sarcastically. "Luke?"

"To be in love, or infatuated?" says Luke.

"Correct. To be beguiled, captivated, entranced, totally head-over-heels in love. From the Latin, *amor*, for *love*. As in 'The beauty was enamored of herself'." He looks at Juliet when he says this – perhaps he does have some redeeming features – but then he continues, directing his next comment at L.J. "It can be used in the negative, too, naturally, as in, 'I am not enamored with your ignorance'."

L.J. merely stares back blankly at him. Maybe he is giving peace a chance.

"As Abraham Lincoln famously said, 'Better to remain silent and be thought a fool than to speak out and remove all doubt', eh, L.J.?"

The class turns as one to look at L.J. He still says nothing, but under his desk his hands are clenched around the metal legs of his desk. The ridges of his knuckles stand out like white pebbles. A muscle pulses in his jaw.

"You know, Mr. Hamel, you could do worse than to follow the example of Luke, here."

"Mr. Perkel –" Luke begins to object as heads swivel to face him, but Perkel holds out a hand to silence him and continues speaking to L.J.

"If you got out in the sun, and got some exercise, you, too, could look healthy and fit."

Luke turns to face L.J., and gives his head a shake as if to distance himself from Perkel's words. He is clearly feeling uncomfortable.

"If *you* put some effort and discipline into your work, as *he* does," Perkel continues, caressing his goatee, "if you just cracked the spine of a book occasionally, then you, too, might be able to answer questions in class."

"Mr. Perkel – *please*," Luke protests, rubbing a hand furiously over the back of his neck.

L.J.'s voice, when he speaks, is soft. It doesn't fit him. Well, maybe it goes with his small head, but not his hulking body.

"Are you going to ask him out on a date soon, if you are so *enamored* of him?"

The class gasps. Perkel's face turns into a pinch-mouthed mask of anger. I burst out into involuntary laughter.

Perkel directs his angry gaze at me. On the distress-inducing scale, it only registers a minor blip. Perhaps being on the singed end of Luke's blazing looks has toughened me up some.

"Was there something you wanted to say, Sloane?"

Now everyone – including L.J., including Luke – is looking at *me*. The wise course would be to mumble a denial and back down apologetically. But this teacher annoys me. He went looking for what he got by picking on L.J. I've been the target of nasty comments often enough to want to stand up to him, too.

"Only that I think comparisons are odious, Mr. Perkel."

"Comparisons are odious?" He's daring me to dig myself into a deeper hole.

I pick up my spade.

"It's another famous saying, though not by Lincoln. It was John Donne, I think. The point is that comparisons between people are often inaccurate and usually counter-productive, because different people have different abilities and interests, and should be judged on their own merits. You shouldn't compare students to each other in terms of work, and certainly not in terms of their physique."

"Are you telling me, in my own classroom, what I should and should not do, young lady?"

Perkel's voice has risen, it sounds high and tight. I look around briefly and see expressions which range from eager to appalled, from doubtful to apoplectic (Perkel's). L.J. is looking at me with an approving smile on his face, as if egging me on. Luke is also looking at me, but his expression is harder to decipher. Then his eyes shift to my scar and he turns back around in his chair. Oh, what the heck …

"Yes, sir. I suppose I am."

My mother would be proud of me.

10

Walking contradiction

Luke

I can't figure her out.

She looks close to cracking most of the time, but then today she took on Perkel – who must be one of the biggest asshats I've ever met – and told him "comparisons are odious". I agreed with that. I had to stop myself nodding and stare at her scar to bring me to my senses.

She wants to swim for fun. Fun! And do her work and take photos and make friends and get on with living her life like she doesn't have a care in the world, but then she gets herself into detention. Deliberately. She stands up to the girls who tease her, but then ducks into the restroom to hide when she sees me coming down the hallway. She walks like she wants no-one to notice her, but still her head sticks out above the other girls. It does that in my brain, too.

Perhaps it's me I can't figure out.

"That's the most fun I've had in English in, like, ages!" Juliet said when our usual crowd gathered at our usual table in the cafeteria for lunch. "I thought the Perkelator was going to cardiac arrest."

"I wish he wouldn't drag me into his beef with L.J. I don't need more trouble in my life," I said. "I don't need more enemies." I give away much too much energy to the ones I already have.

"Poor Lukey!" Juliet gave my arm a consoling squeeze, pulling me against her side and against the softness of her breast. Accidental? Somehow I don't think so. I know she likes me, wants me to ask her out. But my life is complicated enough. And anyway, I don't think she does it for me.

"Why'd you think she did it, though? Sloane, I mean, sticking it to Perkel like that?" Keith asked the question that was puzzling me.

"She wasn't sticking it to Perkel. She was sticking up for L.J." said Juliet.

"But why though?" Exactly. "They're not friends."

"Like attracts like, so freaks gotta stick together."

Everyone in the group laughed, except Keith. And me.

"So, movies and pizza on Friday night, after the game?" Tyrone asked Juliet.

"Sure, let's all go. You coming, Luke?" Juliet asked.

"I'll have to take a rain check. I've got training on Friday night. A coach from Loyola is coming to give us some pointers."

"Come after you're done, then."

"I'll be wasted after that."

Also, I'll need to head home as soon as I can. Dad leaves for a conference on Thursday morning and won't be back until Sunday night, and mom shouldn't be home alone.

"You have no social life at all, Luke! Like, my parents have a better social life than you," said Juliet, looking put out.

Tyrone, on the other hand, looked kind of pleased. He laughed and said, "You're sad, man, sad."

Truth.

11

Rogue thoughts

Both L.J. and I are given a detention for Friday afternoon, which was when I'd planned to go out and take photographs for the L.O. project. My only consolation is that we must have derailed Perkel's plans, too, since he personally supervises our detention, making sure we sit on opposite sides of the otherwise empty classroom and have no opportunity to exchange a word. Maybe he's afraid that if we get together, we may form a dissident anti-Perkel society. Maybe he's not wrong.

When Perkel's back is turned for a minute, L.J. waves to get my attention and then flings something at me. I catch it. It's a stick of "Red-Hot Cinnamon" flavored gum. I grin at him and mouth my thanks, but when I start chewing, it's like eating fire. It's a lucky thing I like spicy. Still, Perkel notices my watering eyes and asks if I'm okay in a tone that tells me he thinks I'm crying because I'm in detention.

"Maybe if I could just go dry my eyes in the restroom?" I ask.

I get a pass from Perkel, and two thumbs-up from L.J.

When I get home, I compulsively scan the news websites and find a new article for my wall of pain. This can be a tricky business. Some of the articles are more likely to trigger a flash of memory or a sudden surge of fear and panic than the relief I want, so I skim through the headlines quickly until I find one so different to my own inner headline, that it's safe to read. "Gator Attack: 'Call 911, my arm is gone'." Perfect. That definitely kicks a red scar to the curb.

Saturday morning starts off with my weekly therapy session. Eileen starts with her usual assessment.

"Flashbacks?"

"Not too many."

"Nightmares?"

"Not really."

"Appetite?"

"I'm eating, sleeping, pooping. All systems are go. I'm ready for take-off."

Eileen smiles and asks me about my week. She listens carefully and I can tell she's proud of me for facing everyone, scar and all.

"You did really well! And it wasn't so bad, now, was it?"

"We-ell …"

"Well?"

"Yes and no."

I tell her about how most people, after the first shocked look, have reacted by studiously not staring at my scar, but how the pack of pretty girls has taken to calling me names. I mention, in a casual, general sort of way, how one boy seems really repulsed by my face, but I can tell she thinks I'm being overly sensitive and so I don't push it. Eileen has keen eyes and even sharper ears, and I'm not ready for her to know how much Luke's attitude has affected me.

The truth is, I'm half-obsessed with him. The delicious infatuation I felt for him before has come back full-force. Only now it's worse, because I see him every day, and can feed my addiction.

I listen to what he says in class and put a check in the block next to "intelligent" on my growing mental list of his attractive attributes. I overhear a conversation between him and his friends and check the box for "funny". I see him training hard every morning and I monitor his times on *Sink-or-Swim*, and my respect grows. Committed? Check. Determined? Check. Talented? You bet. And he's friendly to everyone except me. In fact, he's such an all-round nice guy that his serious aversion to facial deformities stands out oddly. It puzzles me because it doesn't seem to fit with the rest of his character.

Plus, there's a new mystery about him which keeps me watching and brooding. I've noticed that at times he seems to tune out from what's happening around him and his features settle into an expression of sadness. And his rare tweets also don't exactly radiate happiness either. There was one this morning. It had a picture of the floodlit pool with a lone swimmer mid-length, and the caption: *My Friday Night Lights.* No smiley face or ironic hashtag. It struck me as being kind of grim. But what has *he* got to be sad about? He's smart, talented, popular, and really, really hot. All the guys want to be him and all the girls want to be with him.

I'm no exception.

I scan for him in every class, decide where to sit based on where he sits (behind and away from him, wherever possible), and sneak glances at him in the hallways and cafeteria. Luke, by contrast, completely ignores me now. He has not directed a look (filthy or otherwise) my way since that strangely piercing look he gave me during my exchange with Perkel. It's like I don't exist.

I've been swimming before school – why should I avoid the pool because of him? But when he arrives with the rest of the swim team, he always gets into the pool on the other side of where I'm swimming. I've had a little fun with this, changing lanes every day and watching him follow suit. It's like we're playing a game – the opposite of tag.

"Sloane?" Eileen's voice disturbs my thoughts.

There – I've been thinking about him again! I must have fallen silent because she's looking at me curiously. I'm not sure exactly why I don't want to tell her about Luke, just that it is too tender to talk about. Thinking about him is like probing the gap from a lost tooth with your tongue – irresistible, but also painful.

"Hmm?"

"What are you thinking?" This is The Shrink's second-favorite question. Top-of-the-pops is, "What are you feeling?"

"Um … So, I got into trouble with a teacher."

"What happened?"

I tell her the story of my altercation with Perkel in all its detail. I know it's to distract her, and also so I don't accidentally let slip what's really bothering me. I expect her to advise me that it's not wise to get on the wrong side of a teacher, especially in the first week at a new school, but she surprises me.

"I'm glad you stood up to him. Bullies thrive when people stay silent."

Yeah, I know all about this. One of these days I'm going to have to stand up to Luke.

I'm doing so well, Eileen says, that she's happy to see me only every second week. I am on therapy parole and though I'm surprised, I'm also pleased at the vote of confidence.

I spend the rest of the day wandering around town taking photographs for the L.O. project. Ed drops me off at West Lake which, despite its name, is more of a large duck pond. It's also the only lake in town, but I guess calling a lake just "The Lake" would be too stupid, so West Lake it is. I start out by snapping off photographs of some obvious displays of visual pollution: a pile of litter just a few feet from a trash can; an illegible graffiti tag-name spray-painted in luminous greens and yellows on the white wall of a food stand; some scummy foam floating on the water's edge, along with a water bottle and what might be a deflated pink balloon – or something way more disgusting.

After a while, though, I figure it's time to get more creative and I start looking, really looking, at the people and sights around me. What spoils what we see? What defaces beauty and ruins the appearance of something? I take a few shots of a woman sunbed-tanned to the rich orange of a Halloween pumpkin, and then some more of other people in the park. Eileen would be so proud of me – my eyeballs are squarely back in their sockets and looking out at the world. I'm actually having fun when a rogue thought intrudes: what will Luke think of my pics? Suddenly, it's a good time to head home. I get Ed to stop a couple of times en route so I can capture a few more images, and also to get a large pepperoni pizza which we share on the way home after I've cleaned my hands with a wet-wipe. (It's always good to keep Ed's mouth full; that way he can't nag me about learning to drive.)

That evening, I make myself a big mug of coffee and use it to down a handful of vitamins while I upload the images from my camera onto my computer. I look through them carefully, picking out the ones which might be good – and there are some which I think are kind of clever – and deleting the bum ones. I don't tinker with them, though, Photo-shopping feels too much like cheating to me. Though if I could photo-shop my face, I'd do it faster than Luke can swim a length of Butterfly. Which is in under fifteen seconds – I know this because I've surreptitiously timed him at the swim team's morning training sessions.

I print out the photos I like and then, before I log off, I do a quick check of email. Okay, if I'm honest – as honest as an un-photo-shopped portrait – I've been checking my inbox regularly since I gave Luke my email address. Tonight, at last, there's a message from him with an attachment: *VisualPollution.doc*. I force myself to read the attachment first. His essay is really good. He's obviously put some work into it. As covering messages go, his gets a prize for brevity.

S.
Here's my section of LO project.
Yours?
L

I read it a couple of times, decide the "Yours?" means "Where's your section of work, woman?" and isn't an indicator of his confusion over how to sign off the message – yours sincerely, yours unpleasantly, yours when a snowball thrives in hell. But I don't intend to send him my photos before Tuesday's L.O. lesson. I figure him having more time to examine them will lead to him having more negative opinions. Also (jeez, this business of being honest with myself will become a real habit if I don't watch out), I want to see his real reaction.

Yup. Apparently there's still some feeble inner fragment which thinks it can change his mind about me, that longs to hear him say: "Goshdarnit, Sloane, but these pictures show real sensitivity and perspicacity. Anyone who could take shots like this must really be a beautiful person ... er ... despite appearances. Please forgive my previous boorish behavior!"

It's not going to happen. I *know* that in my head. I get my head to speak sternly to the other, less rational parts of me, and go to bed. The rogue thoughts give me no rest there, either.

I dream that I am swimming, as fast as I can, in the school pool. I'm doing an odd mutant stroke which keeps my head submerged in the water but I still somehow know without looking that Luke is swimming ahead of me. It's exhausting swimming like this, especially once we're out in the open ocean. I try to catch up with him, but high waves with crests of foam like broken glass keep pushing me further back. I thrash my legs and arms faster and faster, and then I bump my head on something. I have swum into a drifting patch of pollution – old pictures and amber plastic and dead phones and empty handbags and black tires are floating like a barricade in front of me. I can't get past the trash. There's a large suitcase bobbing on the water near me. Treading water to keep from sinking, I push and shove all the debris into it and tie it up tightly with a rope so it won't burst open. Then I thrust the suitcase behind me and strike out towards Luke, but my leg tangles in the rope and I have to swim on, dragging all this useless garbage behind me. It slows me down. Panicking, I stick my head out of the water and see Luke, who is a dolphin, leaping in and out of the waves, disappearing into the distance.

12

Defaced

Sunday is spent with my aunt Beryl (my mother's younger sister), my uncle Dave, and their two-year-old triplets. I help aunt Beryl with the noisy toddlers and reassure her at least twenty-two times that I'm fine, my new school is just swell, and that yes, I'm making friends – everyone is so kind and welcoming, and the teachers are great. It's probably what she wants to hear. There's a desperate and slightly insane gleam in her eyes that tells me she can't handle more drama, and seeing Devon, Keagan and Teagan trampolining on the sofa – alternately licking melting popsicles and punching one another in the head – I can see why.

Tuesday follows Monday, and L.O. follows History as surely as my eyes follow the back of Luke's head. This is the only view of him I usually have, since he is still ignoring me – protecting his delicate sensibilities by averting his gaze from my unsightly face. But there's no avoiding me now, no sir. Mrs. Copeman tells us to get on with our projects and I take the seat next to Luke as soon as Juliet has vacated it – which she does with a breathy sigh and a longing look at Himself.

"I got your essay," I say to the side of his (unblemished) face. "It was really good. I corrected some of the spelling and changed a few sentences. I hope you don't mind."

Apparently he does. I blanch at the look he gives me. I hand him the corrected print-out of his work and he reads it through – surely noting, but not saying anything about, my changes. When he is finished, he merely nods and then holds out a hand to me. It is a fine hand. I have a thing for hands, and for wrists, and this is a great specimen.

I look at it, swallow, and then look a query at him.

"Your work?" he asks.

"Oh, yes."

I fish the envelope of photographs out of my bag and place it onto the desk in front of him. When he picks it up and takes the photographs out, I have an excuse to stare at his hands again. They are good hands: strong-looking, yet with long slender fingers. Pity he doesn't have hairy pork-sausage fingers, because that right there would put me off him, big-time. And I seriously need to be put off.

I watch him nervously for any reaction while he looks through the first few pictures (the litter, graffiti and scuzzy pond scum) without comment. He pauses when he gets to the picture of a massive McDonalds yellow arch in the heart of West Lake suburbia, then nods and the corner of his mouth twitches. I knew he would get it. I scooch to the edge of my chair to see if he gets the next one. It's of an attractive young woman whose beautiful skin is marked by an amateurish tattoo on her neck and a triple-piercing through her brow.

He studies the picture, holds it up to me and says, "Tattoos as skin pollution? Controversial."

He has turned to face me directly and he isn't scowling. When he comes to the shot of the day-glo orange babe, he actually grins. My stomach does something peculiar deep inside me and I think I might hear the *Hallelujah!* of an angel chorus reverberating inside my head.

"You left this in here," he says, picking out one of the photographs and handing it back to me, while continuing to look through the shots. I look down at the photo. It's the close-up I took of my own face, balancing the camera on a shelf in my wardrobe and using the automatic timer function. I was a bit too close to the lens for the bright flash, so the shot is a touch over-exposed, but it somehow works to the picture's advantage. My skin looks unnaturally white, my eyes a vivid blue, and the slashing scar stands out even more starkly. I hand the picture back to him.

"No, it's … I meant it to be in there."

He glances up from a picture of a fat man's butt-cleavage, his grin fading.

"What?" He looks confused.

"It's an example of, you know, what spoils the visual."

"You …"

He misses a beat, frowns, looks at me oddly.

"Are you kidding me? Jeez!"

"No. I … I thought …"

I don't know what to say. He's angry again.

"I can redo it if you think it's overexposed."

He looks at me as if I'm crazy.

"Or, we can toss it if you don't like it."

"Or," he says, pushing the photo back firmly at me, "we can toss it because it doesn't belong in this collection. Jeez!"

I'm rattled, not sure what he means. I know he hates my scar. He finds it repugnant – he has made that abundantly clear. If anyone can see that it's a visual pollutant, he can.

"The rest of these are pretty good," he says, sounding grudging. "Now we need to get together, I guess, and combine both sections into one document."

"We can do it at my place – I have a scanner and printer and stuff," I volunteer. He nods. "When are you free?"

We agree to meet on Friday afternoon at my apartment to finish the project. I scrawl my address on a piece of paper and give it to him. He hands me the photographs, gives me a long, searching look and turns back to his work.

13

Upside down

Luke

She's nuts.

She actually stuck a picture of herself in the photos of visual pollution. And it wasn't a mistake and she wasn't kidding.

Was she maybe doing it for attention? Did she hope I'd be all don't worry, you're still beautiful, it doesn't matter, forget the past and focus on the future? Not going to happen, Water Baby.

Or does she truly think she's "polluted", that the scar makes her ugly?

Like I said, nuts.

Training was cancelled tonight because half the team's got the flu and coach is away. So I get to go straight home, to spend an extra few hours in the house of fun.

The hall and living room are empty when I arrive, but mom must have heard the door.

"Who's that?"

"It's me." Just me.

I follow the sound of clicking keys to the study. Mom is seated at the desk, a full coffee cup and an empty glass beside her, working on her computer. Another digital album about my golden-boy, Harvard-going, genius brother she'll never finish?

"How was school?" There's no real curiosity in her voice.

"Fine. How are you doing?"

"Good. Today's a good day. I'm keeping busy," she says, her voice brittle with unspoken things. "Look what I've started: *Andrew's early years!*"

I walk around the desk to peer over her shoulder at the screen. Andrew sitting in a stroller, his mouth plugged with a pacifier; Andrew taking his first steps; Andrew and I kicking a ball around in the back yard.

"What do you think?" She turns her thin face up to me, desperate for something I can't give her.

"It's great, mom. Your best yet."

"I think so, too."

Her smile is faint and fades quickly. Mom used to have such a great smile, and a deep, musical laugh which usually ended in hiccups. It hurts to see this pale imitation on her cracked lips.

"Can I get you anything, something to eat maybe?" I ask. "You should eat something."

"I'm not hungry."

There's a skin on top of her cold coffee.

"A fresh cup of coffee?"

She shakes her head and leans into the screen again. "Such a cute little boy."

"I think this one is me," I say, pointing at the picture of a smiling boy, maybe five or six years old, standing on his head.

"Are you sure? Andrew had it in his room."

"Yeah, it's me. I was always the upside-down kid." Still am, in a way.

"Oh, well, if you're certain," she sighs and deletes the photo from the page.

I stare at the black-framed white space for a moment, then kiss the top of her head and leave her to her world.

14

First touch

On Friday, I rush home after school to get there before Luke does. I have high hopes for this afternoon in the continuing campaign to convert Luke into seeing past my face and acknowledging the beautiful human being lurking beneath. Since our L.O. lesson on Tuesday, he has been less frosty towards me. He's not friendly, precisely, but he definitely has thawed a little in the iciness stakes. I switch on the PC so it can start booting up, get a pot of coffee going, then dart around the small apartment hanging up towels and clothes, and putting away my dried breakfast dishes.

The buzzer for the apartment block entrance goes off as I'm shoving my bottles of nail polish into the already stuffed bathroom cabinet. I shut the door against the impending avalanche of make-up, moisturizer and shampoo bottles, and run to the intercom at the door. I buzz him up, and force myself to wait three seconds after he rings the doorbell before I open the door.

The air is sucked out of me again. I always forget just how good-looking he is, so that it sandbags me every time we come face to face. Today he is wearing black sneakers, faded jeans, and a white T-shirt with a small hole on the seam of one shoulder. My index finger itches to push through it and touch the skin beneath.

"May I come in?"

I realize I've been standing there, just staring.

"Of course."

I step aside to let him in, surreptitiously wiping my mouth with the back of my hand to check for drool. He passes me, and I catch a whiff of something that smells faintly of spice. And of him.

He stares at the line of newspaper articles stretching along the wall.

"You have a thing for the really good news, I see?"

He has a lopsided almost-grin on his face. I shrug, wishing I'd thought to take them down.

"They motivate me," I say.

He looks perplexed.

'You're motivated by people who are attacked and burned and," he peers closer to read a headline, "-dismembered?"

"Uh-huh."

I want to explain it to him, but he's already turning away, muttering something under his breath. It's clear he thinks I'm mentally deranged - he might be right on that score. He looks around as we walk into the living room, and glances down the hallway that leads to my bedroom and the bathroom.

"You live here with …?"

"I live alone."

He turns to face me at that.

"Like, alone-alone?"

"Yup. Um … would you like something to drink? A soda, or some coffee?"

"Coffee would be great. Thanks," he says, rubbing a hand behind his neck. I'm not the only one feeling awkward.

I go to the kitchen, and set out a tray with the coffee pot, milk, sugar, cups and spoons. I bought some cookies for today and I put these on a plate, but they look stupid – as if I neatly arranged them. So I carefully order them into a careless jumble, then I pick up the tray and head back to the living room.

Luke is moving along the tall rack of shelves that covers the length of one wall. He runs a hand over the spines of my books as he studies their titles, then moves on to my small collection of fossilized ammonites, picking one up in his long fingers and turning it over to examine it. Meanwhile, I'm examining the back of him. His hair is cut short, like all the boys on the swim team, but it twists into a point at the top of his neck. I can see the line of his broad swimmer's shoulders and the lean muscles of his back under his T-shirt. The view of his denim-clad rear is not too much of a trial for my eyes either.

He leans forward to look closer at my display of medals, trophies and plaques from when I used to swim competitively, and the framed, gold-bordered certificate of my advanced life-saving qualification. I must make some noise, because he turns to face me. There's a sad smile on his face which literally makes my mouth fall open, it's so beautiful.

"You were good," he says.

I shrug and nod, put the tray down on the coffee table. Will he sit next to me on the sofa while we have our coffee? He turns back to the shelf, moving along to a photo of my mother. It's an enlarged close-up of her face that I took on her old camera when we were on a rare vacation at the beach. She never took much time off from work, so when we did get away together, we always made the most of it. I was fourteen that summer, but that didn't stop me from exploring the tide-pools with her, plastic bucket and net in hand, like a little kid. In the picture, her face is slightly flushed with sunburn and she's smiling widely, looking happy and carefree. Other memories of her – more recent ones – threaten to bubble up to the surface, but I push them behind the curtain of now.

"That's my moth-"

"I know who it is," he says, turning to face me. His face is tight again, his eyes hard.

"Let's just get to work, okay?" he snaps.

I'm muddled by the abrupt change in him. I need to confront him and I'll do it, too, just as soon as I get my breath back.

We each grab a cup of coffee – he takes his black, like his freaking mood, I notice – and then sit down at the corner desk where the computer is. He casts a disparaging look at the bottles of vitamins and immune-boosters clustered beside my screen that I forgot to hide in my hurried tidy-up. On top of them, embarrassingly, lies a thermometer. Flushing, I push them aside, pulling the keyboard closer and tilting the screen so that he can see.

We begin to work. I grab the mouse and do the cutting, pasting, scanning and merging; he offers suggestions and comments – all of them strictly related to our project. He sits so close, as he studies the screen, that I can feel the heat coming off his body. It makes my hands clumsy on the keyboard. I'm grateful to the programming geeks in Silicon Valley who invented auto save, because twice I nearly succeed in wiping out the whole project. I'm also made edgy – half upset and half angry – by the tension which radiates off of him. It's clear he'd rather be anywhere but here. I'm working as fast as I can, but we still have a way to go when it happens.

I'm leaning across him to catch a piece of paper as it emerges from the mouth of the printer, when I accidentally brush against him. My bare arm just touches his. He flinches and pulls back as if I've burnt him, or something. That's it – I've had just about as much as I can take.

"So sorry," I say in a voice dripping with false sweetness. "I forgot."

"You forgot?" There is ice in the fire of his hazel eyes now.

"Yes! I forgot to be careful not to touch you – in case I *contaminate* you, in case my face is contagious. I forgot that there are people in the world who are obsessed with appearance and are just plain rude when it comes to those of us who look a little less than perfect!"

I'm almost shouting as I fling the paper onto the desk and face him head on.

"*What?*"

Unbelievably, he – *he!* – sounds outraged. If anyone's got dibs on justifiable moral outrage here, it's damn well me.

"Didn't your mother ever tell you that it's rude to stare at people with disfigurements? You're rude! And offensive."

"*Me? I* offend *you*?" Again with that tone of indignant anger. It fuels my own rage.

"Yes you are! I mean, what is your problem? I'm scarred, alright? It's ugly – I know that. Actually, I know it better than you do. But there's not a damn thing I can do about it, Okay? And – newsflash! – I never asked for it. If I offend you *so* much, perhaps you should keep your eyes closed. Or explain to Mrs. Copeman that I physically nauseate you and demand a new partner on the grounds of physical health. Juliet looks keen, and there's nothing wrong with *her* face."

Luke stares at me, his face blank with something like shock. He opens his mouth to speak, starts to say something, stops, then tries again.

"You think I'm offended by your *face*? That I'm upset by your scar?"

"Aren't you?"

Now I'm the one who is surprised. It derails my anger.

"No, I'm not. It's not how you look, it's who you are, *that* you are. As soon as Perkel told the class your name, I knew who you were."

"But –" I splutter, "I don't understand. You hardly know me. How can you be so mortally offended by who I am?"

"My name is Luke Naughton, Sloane."

I'm trying hard to understand what he means, even as a corner of my mind registers that this is the first time he's said my name, that it makes his mouth move in interesting ways.

"I know that," I say.

"Luke *Naughton*."

It's clear this is supposed to mean something to me, but it doesn't. I stare uncomprehendingly back at him.

"Brother of Andrew Naughton." His voice is bitter with cold fury.

My scalp creeps back over my head. Something dreadful is happening.

"Ah, rings a bell, does it?"

"Ohhh." I realize who he is. "Oh!"

I understand everything now, understand him. It feels like someone pulled a plug on the bottom of my feet; I can feel the blood draining from my face, my knees giving way. I need to sit, to get out of the range of those accusing, icy eyes.

"Oh ..." the last of my breath escapes on the soft syllable.

What a fool I've been to hope, to dream, when my life has taught me so brutally that the good stuff's not for me. And him! How must he have felt these last weeks, trapped in a classroom, on a project, with me – living, breathing, walking, talking me? Constantly faced with my scar – the revolting reminder of what he has lost.

"I ... I ..."

I don't know what to say. I sag onto the sofa, bury my face in my hands, mumble, "I didn't know, Luke. I never knew who you were, that you were at this school. I would never have –"

I'm interrupted by a snort. I look up to see his retreating back. He stalks out of the room, wrenches the front door open so hard it bangs against the wall, then slams it shut behind him.

There's an ache in my chest, an actual physical heart-ache, as I sit in the sudden silence, staring at the closed door in front of me.

And then it all surges upwards, all the memories I've been holding back and pressing down and trying to breathe away. And it's enough to drown me.

15

A fierce cold burn

I was sixteen years old the day I got the scar, and everything changed.

Where I live, west of Chicago, it's hot and humid in the summer. Heat hazes shimmer in the distance and the roads steam when thunderstorms rip through the city and suburbs, lashing the trees, hurling fat raindrops down and sizzling the air with cracks of lightning. You can smell the storms coming. There's a trace of ozone in the air, like the promise of love – sweet and exhilarating and dangerous. When the afternoon light turns lime, a bad one is on the way. After the world has been sluiced clean and threatened with destruction, the sun blazes again. Winters start cold and then get colder. When the sun shines, it does so with pallid weakness and it retreats like a coward to the coming of snow.

That day – *the* day – was just another cold November school morning. It began ordinarily enough: mom nagging me awake with threats that I'd be late, the mad scramble to shower, dress and pack my bag. I was still chewing on a breakfast bar as I climbed into the car, tossing my bags into the tiny rear seat. The lack of room for friends at the back was only one of the things I hated about mom's "new" car – a 1969 Aston Martin DB6 Vantage – which had been her fortieth birthday present to herself. I also disliked the right-hand drive, the noisy engine, the tiny trunk and the fact that it was stick-shift. But mom loved the sleek silver styling, the wooden steering wheel, the luscious red leather interior and the powerful six-cylinder engine. She said the classic coupe made her feel like James Bond. I said it made her drive like him, too.

Mom swore under her breath as we belted up.

"We're late already, and we still have to stop on the way to get the painting."

"What painting?"

"The painting for the office. We've had one of the boardroom paintings reframed and I want it up on the wall in time for this morning's partners' meeting."

"Does it have to be you who picks it up? Can't you send some assistant to get it?" I mean, what's the point of being a senior partner in a law firm if you can't get flunkies to do your bidding?

"It's on our way, Sloane. Besides, I want to check that –"

"– that it's perfect!" I completed the sentence for her.

"Am I so predictable?" Mom smiled at me.

"Just a little." I grinned back.

The rain was falling more heavily now, slowing down the morning traffic and stressing my mother even more. The weatherman had predicted snow before the weekend.

"Chill, mom," I said, and pulled out my cell phone to check on my messages and mail.

"I hate to be late," said my mother, and stretched out a hand automatically to reach into her handbag as the shrill ring of her phone sounded.

"Mom, don't." I hated it when my mother used the phone while driving.

"Lana Munster," she answered, pulling a face at me. "... Yes, I'm on my way in ... Of course, I have the contracts ... As soon as I can, okay? I should be another ..." she cradled the phone between her jaw and shoulder so that she could glance at her wristwatch, and took her other hand off the wheel to turn down the radio as we took off from the traffic lights. And they say teenagers are bad drivers!

"... another thirty minutes, just need to get the painting and drop Sloane off ... I'll *be* there, okay? Bye."

She ended the call with her thumb and tossed the phone into her bag, glaring at the traffic in front of her and trying to find a gap to get into the lane closest to the sidewalk. The wipers swished clear streaks across the windshield, and the headlights shone shafts of light into the glittering downpour.

"I wish you wouldn't do that, mom. You know it's dangerous."

They had shown us a video, in driver's ed., showing how distracted cellphone users were. Worse than driving drunk, the instructor said.

"Oh, lighten up, Sloane! You're sixteen, not sixty. Who's the mother around here?" She flipped her scarf – a bright stream of coral and crimson and butter-yellow – over her shoulder.

"Right, the framing store's coming up – look for a parking spot ... There!"

She pulled over and into a diagonal space near a store with the name "Frame of Mind" in gold lettering on the front window. It still looked dark inside the store.

"Are they even open yet?"

"For me – naturally!" said my mother.

She was out of the car and in the store moments later. My mother had to do everything at speed. I guess it was part of the drive and determination that had fuelled her career success. Well, that and the awareness that as a single parent, all the responsibility for providing for us was on her shoulders. I tried to remember this when I got irritated by her inability ever to switch off from work, to ignore the phone, to relax and spend time with me.

I checked my make-up in the visor mirror, then fiddled with the radio – one of the few things that had been updated in the car – and found a song I liked: "Give me Love" by Ed Sheeran. I had just closed my eyes to enjoy the music when there was a hammering at my window. Mom was there, holding a large painting and gesturing to me to open my door. When I did, she thrust the painting onto my lap and then ran around to her side of the car.

"Why do I have to hold it? Why can't it go on the back seat?" I whined.

"Because it might fall and break the glass. Just hold it tight, will you?" Mom started the engine and backed up at speed out of the parking space. Behind us a car horn honked in protest.

"And wipe the rain off it," said Mom, reaching her arm over to brush the droplets of water off the glass and pale wood frame with her sleeve. I shoved her arm away.

"Both hands on the wheel, Mom, focus!" I said. "And buckle up already."

"Let me just get into the stream of traffic here. You okay, there?"

"I've been more comfortable."

The painting was big and bulky. It pressed heavily into my thighs and obscured my portion of the windshield. I tried to maneuver it flat, so that it would lie more comfortably on my lap. I could only manage to rest it on a slant between my stomach and the dashboard, but I could at least see where we were going. I was glad the rain was lightening up, because when my hair got damp, it got frizzy. The frame of the painting was poking into my stomach and I shifted it a little. Now my midriff was pushed up against it. I looked down at the picture critically, pulling a face at the boring, empty landscape, painted in dull olives and browns, devoid of any humans or animals.

"This will brighten up your boardroom no end," I said. "I can see why it was so important to get it reframed and on the wall. A real cheerful conversation piece, this is." Before she could interrupt and tell me it was very valuable and tasteful, I continued, "Listen, Mom, there's something I've been wanting to ask you."

"Now?"

"Yes, now. No time like the present – isn't that what you're always saying? Are you listening?"

"I always listen, Sloane."

I rolled my eyes. She always listened to several things at once, heard maybe half of them.

"I wanted to ask you for –" I began, but my mother's phone was summoning her again; this time it was the double-tone that indicated an incoming text message. Her hand dipped again into her bag and fished out the phone. She pressed a button automatically, looked down to read the message.

We were coming up to an intersection where the traffic lights shone in shimmering amber pools on the rain-wet road. Out of habit I scanned the road ahead. And saw several things at once. Traffic lights turning red, cars in the lanes adjacent to us stopping, two kids in school uniforms starting to run across the road in front of us.

I wanted to yell, "Mom, lookout! Stop! It's red. There's someone in front. Stop!" but all I got out was "Mah!"

In the same instant, I reached out my hand and grabbed the steering wheel, yanking down hard. The car slewed to the side – just avoided hitting the two little girls. In my peripheral vision, I saw the smaller one stumble forward. The car had just nudged the bag on her back, but they were safe. We had missed them. In the fraction of a second it took to register this fact, the car travelled into the intersection. I guess Mom must have slammed her foot on the brake, I don't know, but we were still moving. I looked up into the wide, round eyes of the driver in the blue car now crossing directly in front of us in the intersection.

There was a deafening, shuddering bang.

And then nothing.

When I opened my eyes, it felt like that bang was still reverberating in my chest. There was a thudding and a pulsing deep inside. My heart? My head felt too heavy to move it from where it rested on my chest. As I lifted it, something slid off my head and fell. I looked down. Lying in the puddle of glass fragments which filled my lap was the remains of the painting – all splintered ends of snapped wooden frame and torn folds of warped canvas. Some long, sharp shards of glass still clung to the edges of the frame, reaching up into the air like crystal stalagmites, and red paint trickled down from one corner across the painting. Why had they framed it when the paint was still wet?

My hands and arms were covered with a layer of rough, round beads of glass; they rolled off when I lifted my arms. Rain was blowing into the car now. I could feel it on my face. It was raining in the car? That would ruin the painting. Mom would not be pleased.

Mom.

There was a moment of realization, a beat, then my heart gave a hard kick and I seemed to come awake.

"Mom!"

I turned to check on her. There was no-one in the seat next to me. An icy swoop turned my stomach cold, colder than the rain blowing in my face as I looked from the empty seat to where the windshield ought to be. A web of crumpled glass hung from the buckled frame, but the part above the steering wheel had been thrust out over the hood of the car.

I shoved the painting aside. It fell into the foot-well, onto the brake and gas pedal, and alongside a cellphone whose screen was still glowing. A part of my mind registered that the screen-saver had not yet had time to kick in. It could only have been seconds since the text came in.

I fumbled to release the catch of the seatbelt; it shook in my hands. I had to get out. My door wouldn't open. I pushed and shoved, checked it was not locked, shoved again. *Must get out!* I pulled back, then, holding the handle open, bashed against the door with my shoulder. It hurt – a sharp pain to join the other pains which I was only now aware of feeling. I felt it as though from a distance, as though I could feel what was happening in someone else's body, as though I weren't in my own.

I couldn't think clearly. My mind was in my throat, where a single word was stuck, unable to force its way past the noose of fear that strangled me. It shrieked inside me. "Mom! Mom! Mom-mom-mom-mom!"

Someone – a woman – was at the door, pulling it open for me, helping me climb out, asking me something. I tried to stand up and crumpled to the ground. There was something wrong with my knee – it would not straighten, would not hold me up. I looked around from where I half-sat, half-lay on the road. The rain was still coming down as it had before, as if nothing had happened, as if the world had not just careened to a stop. Smoke, or perhaps it was steam, was rising in a cloud from under the arched hood of our car. The other car, a twisted mangle of blue, had spun off to one side but my eyes were riveted at once to a flash of sunset colors, part of a crumpled heap lying impossibly far away from our car. Leaning on the woman, I hobbled across the rough, wet surface of the road, towards that blaze of crimson and orange.

There's a gap, an absence in my memory here. And then I am back inside the moment but outside of myself, looking dispassionately from a little way away as that girl who is also me sits on the road, with my mother's head in her lap, paying no attention to the people who are milling all around. My mother's eyes are open, but dull. There is an absence in them, too. And the me outside of me knows that she is gone, knows that the flattening on the side of her head must constitute a fatal injury. There is no point in trying CPR, my logical mind deduces. Instead, I should get up, go and check the other car – surely that driver needs help. I must call 911, phone my mother's office and let them know she will not be in today.

But even as these thoughts race through my mind, the other part of me – the part inside my bowed body – hangs onto my mother, tries to shake a light into her staring eyes, cradles her head between my hands as the scream finally breaks through my tight throat.

"Mommmm!"

The blood on my mother's cheek is washed away by the falling rain and reappears fresh and red. A puddle of blood stains the lap of my jeans. My mother must be bleeding from her head wound, I reason, I should stop shaking her – it could make her worse. *Foolish*, the rational part outside chides me, *a stopped heart cannot pump blood*. The blood, it points out, cannot be coming from my mother. It must be coming from me. The drops are coming quickly now, the rain cannot wash the crimson splashes off her waxy white face quickly enough.

I lift my right hand to my face, feel a strange gaping sensation. As I touch it, I become aware of the pain there. A fierce cold burn.

The edges of my vision are suddenly ragged, as if they are being nibbled by the blackness beyond.

My hand comes away from my face covered in red. But the pool of blood staining my jeans, spreading out from beneath my thighs to frame my mother's face like a blossoming red halo, must be coming from somewhere other than this steady trickle falling from my face onto hers. It must also be coming from me, from my upper thigh. *Heavy bleeding,* the logical voice chips in, *that's bad.*

It is drifting further away, that voice, but so am I. The black tugs at me, and I want to go, to leave here and be enveloped by its nothingness.

But now someone else is crouched down in front of me. I can't quite make him out. He is blurry and he sways. He holds my shoulder, says something in a loud voice – words I can't make out.

I try to tell him the important things: to tell him to check the other car, and also that I'm bleeding from somewhere, and that my mom …

But the gnawing darkness opens its maw and swallows me whole.

16

B.S. and A.S.

B.S. and A.S. That's how I divide my life: Before Scar and After Scar.

I say "scar", although of course, there were many. But it's the one that matters.

There were many things I had planned to do in my life – before I got the scar, I mean. And some of them were going to take me out of my city and into the wide world out there.

I was going to swim better than I ever had before. I was a pretty good swimmer. Backstroke and breaststroke – those were my thing. I'm tall, and my long arms and legs gave me an advantage over the other girls in the water. I was going to swim for the regional zone team – had just, in fact, qualified at the trials. Next stop would be sectionals, then nationals, and maybe even the Olympics, one day. It was a long-shot, a dream, but not entirely beyond the bounds of possibility. And it's not a big-enough dream if it's easy, right?

Plus, I was dedicated. Monday to Friday, I arrived at the training center's heated pool at 5a.m. so I could get in a good two-and-half hours of training before school. There were another two hours every afternoon or evening – strength training and speed work – and five hours each on Saturday and Sunday. I was a regular on the competition circuit, pitting myself against the best in my category, collecting medals like stepping stones on the path to becoming number one.

Before I got the scar, I had also planned to look up my dad and reconnect with him. My parents had divorced when I was just five years old and I could remember only bits of him: the scratch of his beard on my cheek when he hugged me, a distinctive sour-sweet smell, the whirl of color when he lifted me over his head and spun me around, the harsh shouts when he and mom fought and I hid among the dirty laundry and damp towels in the bottom of the large bathroom closet.

Mom was unusually cagey on the reasons behind their breakup and the reason he wasn't a feature in my life, but she had agreed I could track him down and make contact once I was sixteen. In these days of Facebook and LinkedIn, how hard could it be to find him? It would be good to get to know him, to begin a relationship from scratch, to hear about his life. I wrote it high up on my to-do list.

I was also, B.S., going to ask my mother something important. I began asking her that rainy day on the drive to school, but her phone beeped before I could get the words out. And that's when everything changed.

Oh, and I was going to meet the cute guy. Definitely.

He was a swimmer too. He swam in the open section, but he still looked young – maybe seventeen or eighteen. He was tall, at least 6'2", with caramel-colored hair, a ripped, abtacular body, and gentle eyes – the kind that made your knees melt, your brain go soft and your stomach clench.

We had made contact in the chat rooms on the Sink-or-Swim! website. On a few occasions, at some trial or swim meet, we'd exchanged glances and smiles. Once he'd handed me my swim meet program when I dropped it, and at the last meet I ever competed in, I almost met him. We had both won our races and after his second event, he pulled himself out of the pool and, still dripping wet, headed over to where I sat on the bleachers. He wrapped a towel loosely around his waist and spoke. To me.

"Hi."

"Hi, yourself." (I've always been one for scintillating conversation.)

"I'm Luke. I think we've met online. I'm *Not_A* – you're *WaterBaby*?"

He had an amazing smile – slow and lazy and just the slightest bit lopsided.

"No. Yes! I mean..." That smile was distracting me, making me stammer and blush, making my brain stutter. "My actual name's –"

"Luke! C'mon, quickly – you're supposed to be on the winner's podium to get your medal."

A coach swept him away while I looked on.

"See you later, Water Baby," he called over his shoulder, but he didn't – not that day at least. Mom had to rush back to the office for an evening meeting, and so we left before the end of the swim meet. All okay, I consoled myself, there were more competitions scheduled before the end of the season and I'd catch him at one of those. Yeah right, so much for that plan.

Many things actually happened after I got the scar, in the time of A.S.

Pretty much straight away, I was dropped from the regional zone team. I had missed the training camp – I was too busy getting blood transfusions, shivering on a stainless steel table in an operating theatre, trying to eat disgusting hospital food, taking meds for my messed up insides, and weeping. Endlessly weeping for my mother.

When my body had recovered enough to be discharged from the hospital, when the stitches had been pulled out of my face and inner thigh, and the brace removed from my knee (now held together with a titanium pin), I went back to the water. I could still swim. I was probably still better than most people in the water, but I couldn't swim well enough to be competitive. I enjoyed being in the water, but I did not race. My knee would never again work as well as it should, and something had gone missing from me – my hunger for the dream, my drive to do much of anything.

I no longer have a grand ambition for my life. Somehow, I don't think I'm going to live too long, anyway. And I'm okay with that.

I did look up my father. To be strictly accurate, the lawyers now administering the trust fund which my mother left me were instructed to trace him, and trace him they did. The search was not easy, apparently, but Bradley, Bradley and Martinez were persistent. They found him on several databases which black-listed bad creditors, and discovered that he had filed for bankruptcy – twice – and was wanted for a string of outstanding debts. Eventually their investigator found him living in the YMCA in Des Moines, Iowa, and a social worker appointed by the state to investigate my circumstances drove me out to meet him.

I introduced myself to the stranger, shook his hand and immediately felt sullied by the smarmy charm of him, the long, dirty fingernails at the ends of his tobacco-stained fingers, the oily excuses for a lifetime of absence, and the now-identified familiar whiff of alcohol emanating from pores and breath as he leaned over to try embrace his "long-lost daughter". He was too oblivious of my life, too uncaring about the loss of my mom, way too interested in my trust fund. On the spot, he listed half a dozen opportunities for once-in-a-lifetime investment prospects. On the spot, I decided I would be better off as far away from him as I could get. Bradley, Bradley and Martinez filed for my legal emancipation from him and I was duly "divorced" from my father. It took a restraining order, though, to get him to stay away and stop contacting me.

The social worker who assessed me told the judge that I was extremely mature for my age and used to caring for myself. The pile of money that Mom left me, her sole heir, meant that I could buy a small unit in the same secure apartment complex in which my aunt Beryl, my mother's younger sister, lived with her toddler triplets and husband. The court agreed that I could live alone as long as I stayed under the regular supervision of my aunt, and received monthly visits from social services. It worked out well; the triplets kept my aunt perpetually busy and out of my hair, so I was left pretty much alone to do my own thing.

It suited me to be alone, to hide out from the world, to finish my second-to last year of school with the help of private tutors and tests written under the eagle-eyes of independent examiners at the lawyers' offices.

A.S., I never needed to ask my mother that question after all, I got what I wanted in a roundabout way. Who needs an increase in their allowance when you inherit your mother's entire estate? Beware what you ask the gods, as they may grant it you, and all that. In my crazier moments, I think I may somehow have caused the accident, willed it into existence by wanting more money. Eileen, the therapist I was sent to after the accident and mom's death to help with the flashbacks and nightmares and anger and grief, had a theory about this.

"It's a kind of magical thinking, a misguided attempt to convince yourself that you had some control (even in a negative direction) over a devastating event in which you were actually completely powerless," she told me.

I was skeptical. Why would I have *wanted* to cause the crash?

"Life's scary when you realize how much of it is out of your control."

That part, I agreed with.

A.S., I spent a lot of time trying to learn how to live with, and around, and in spite of the empty holes that now took up the space where my mother had been. It amazed me, I mean really and truly staggered me, how life went on all around me even though it felt like my life had stopped. Dogs still barked, phones rang, hamburgers came off the grill in a stream at McDonalds, and people lined up – in the drive-through and at the counter – they lined up to buy the stuff. People actually still wanted to eat.

How could anyone have an appetite when my mom was gone? Not there in the mornings to nag me awake, or there in the middle of the night when I had the flu, or beside me in the car laughing at a comedy sketch on the radio. Where had she gone? How was it possible that all of her – not just her body, but her stories and memories, had been obliterated? Gone. Gone somewhere I could never get them. Things she had never told me about herself, I would never now know.

And the world simply marched on as if this was a regular old thing.

"In the midst of life we are in death," the minister had said at the funeral.

But it seemed to me, rather, that in the midst of death we are in life. Somehow, I was undeniably – obscenely even – alive. After a while, I even got hungry again and I ate, staying clear of the tastes that had been Mom's favorites: sushi and fresh lemonade and homemade mac 'n cheese. I ate, alone for the most part, looking at the empty chair across the table and thinking of Mom, and thinking, too, of that other family somewhere that was missing a member. His name was Andrew. They didn't tell me much, but they told me that.

I had not been well enough to attend the inquest. My witness statement was submitted by affidavit. The lawyers said that the family of the dead man had been there, determined to see justice done. It was, and it wasn't. My mother was held responsible for causing the accident through driving while using the phone, but she was not around to take her punishment. Or, looking at it another way, she had paid the ultimate price: a death sentence for accidentally taking the life of another. Messrs. Bradley and Martinez tried to protect me from all that, though they reluctantly agreed to pass on a letter of condolence that I wrote to the family. I was allowed to express regret but not to apologize because, according to the lawmen, that would open me to lawsuits. That time is all a bit hazy now, a series of unconnected images remembered through the mists of pain meds and grief. I always knew that one day I would need to meet that family in person, but the thought of it scared me stupid. Turns out, I was right to be afraid.

So that's how I've spent the nine months since I got the scar – recovering and sleeping and crying and hiding. And even eating – though only after I've washed or wiped my hands. And, in spite of myself, living. More or less.

And, of course, A.S. – I've finally met the cute guy.

17

Ground zero

Luke

I don't know what makes me maddest.

That I've had to suffer her presence these last weeks, knowing who she is while she's been living in ignorant bliss?

That she's been living, when Andrew is dead?

That she thought I was the sort of guy who would hate a girl because she's *scarred*?

Or that she didn't even remember his name! Oh yeah, that's the one. That's what enrages me most. She didn't even remember Andrew's name.

All this time, she's been happily getting on with her life, forgetting his name – hell, forgetting his death, for all I know – while mom and dad and I have been stuck at ground-zero.

I actually began to feel sorry for her when I saw how she lived – all alone with the reminders of the past on her shelves, and all those clippings of other peoples' tragedies. It was weird. And a bit sad. I guess I understood for the first time that she'd lost her mother. And I kind of know what that feels like.

But then she was all *you're rude, I can't help my face!* And I was blown away because I suddenly realized she didn't even know I was Andrew's brother. She didn't even remember his name. And then there was no more room inside me for *sorry.* I was too full of fury.

I wish there was such a thing as a pain-transplant. I'd like to collect all the Naughton tears and silence and hurt and pack it into her. Let her see what pain feels like. I need to punish someone, but her mother checked out at the very moment she killed Andrew and ended the family we once had. Because Andrew took all the good stuff when he left, no doubt about it. Only the husks of us were left behind, rattling around the house where Andrew isn't anymore.

Dad is crushed. Mom is ... I don't even have words for what mom is. And I'm trapped here, a skin of rage and guilt and grief stretched tight around a great big hole where my brother and my family and my old life used to be.

Tonight I'm going to train until I'm so tired I can't feel a thing. And tomorrow I'm bringing my Banjo home. I don't care what mom and dad say. Andrew might be the one who's dead, but we're the ones who live in a morgue, and I can't handle the lifeless silence that is our house any more.

18

Cuts and bruises

It's the Saturday morning after the Friday night confrontation with Luke and I'm going to spend the morning with Sienna, doing some shopping downtown before catching a movie.

She takes one look at my face and asks, "Oh you poor thing! Are you sick?"

"No," I say. Do I look that bad?

"Maybe you have hay fever or allergies or something."

"Nope, no allergies."

"But your eyes are red and puffy and your face looks kind of swollen." She tilts her head to take in all my glory, her dark eyes are full of concern.

"I'm not sick, I've just been crying. A lot." This is no understatement. It's been – I consult my watch – sixteen hours, off and on.

"Why? Has something happened? Is it a boy?" she asks. Rabid curiosity has replaced the concern in her expression.

We go into a coffee shop and over an iced mochaccino (me), a hot chocolate (her) and two enormous slices of cheesecake (we both need our protein), I tell her how I got my scar in a car accident.

"I wondered, but I never wanted to ask. I thought you'd tell me when you were ready," Sienna says.

I tell her everything. The accident. My mother. The other driver. My injuries. The last year. And Luke Naughton. She is shocked, but she responds just as a real friend should – with compassion and understanding and reassurances.

"It was an accident, Sloane, it was nobody's fault. Sometimes dreadful things just happen."

"Yes, it was an accident, but my mother was trying to text on her cellphone at the time, Sienna, she was negligent. She wasn't looking and she went through a traffic light that had already turned red."

"Oh," says Sienna. Right, oh. "That's … bad."

"Yeah, and it gets worse. It's really my fault. I'm the one who made our car hit the other car."

I tell her about how I saw the two school kids in the road in front of us, how I yanked on the steering wheel and sent us straight into the other car – straight into Andrew Naughton.

"Well …" she says and pauses to take a long sip of her hot chocolate. I know she's buying time, trying to think of what to say. But, really, there is nothing to say. It is what it is.

"It's a tragedy," she says and I nod. It's freaking tragic alright, no doubt about that.

"But you're not to blame, and it's wrong of Luke to blame you. You were trying to avoid an accident, to *not* kill someone. If you hadn't turned the wheel, two kids might now be dead."

I shrug. I've spent days and nights trying to figure out the various permutations of "what if?" It doesn't change anything. My mother is dead. Andrew Naughton is dead – because of my mother and because of me. And I'm alive. Luke Naughton resents that and hates me.

"And look what he tweeted last night." I show her the latest of Luke's infrequent tweets.

There are no words for this.

"You think that's about you? About what happened last night?" Sienna asks.

I shrug unhappily.

"It must be really tough having to work together on that project."

"You have no idea. On Monday, I'm going to try to get Copeman to allow us to change partners. She already said 'no' once, but maybe if she knows how things are, she'll cut him some slack."

"And you, too" says Sienna.

"What?"

"This is not an easy situation for you, either, Sloane."

That's true, but I reckon it's a cakewalk for me compared to what it must be like for him. And although he hasn't been understanding, let alone forgiving, I don't feel like I'm entitled to kid gloves from him. Not after what I've done. Not given who I am. I try to shake myself out of the heaviness that constricts my chest and pushes down on my shoulders. I call for the check and pay.

"Do you mind if we pop into the drugstore before the movie? There are a couple of things I need to get."

"Sure," she says and we head out.

In the drugstore, Sienna goes to examine the cosmetic counters while I grab a shopping basket and fill it with antibacterial soap dispensers, antiseptic throat sprays, germ-killing cleaners for my kitchen and bathroom, three tubes of vitamin C fizzy tablets, and half-a-dozen travel packs of anti-bacterial wipes. You can never have too many anti-bacterial wipes. I'll use up a whole pack at the movies alone, between wiping the arm-rests, the toilet seat, flusher handle and door-latch, and schools are a hotbed of sources of infection.

I check on Sienna. She has several red and pink lipstick stripes on her left wrist and is now happily sniffing at different perfume samples. I head to the back of the store, where a registered nurse runs a Saturday clinic, weighing babies and giving them their vaccinations, testing blood sugar levels for diabetics, checking the blood pressure of old folks and talking to embarrassed teens about contraception. I'm in luck. There's no line and I can go straight in.

It's a small consulting room, with an examination table on one side and a set of baby scales under a hanging musical mobile on the other. Nurse Linda sits behind a desk on which there are two large, glass jars; one is filled with green lollipops, and the other with foil-wrapped condoms.

"Better be sure not to mix up those bottles, Linda," I say, "or the kids will get disappointed and the boys will get –"

"Sloane!" she interrupts in happy surprise. "How are you?"

"Good, fine. How are you?"

"Oh, I'm always well. How have you been? Staying healthy?"

"Yup. No infections. My temperature was up a bit a few days ago, but I've been taking vitamin C and Echinacea and I've been fine since. I think it's time to get my flu shot, though."

I hop onto the examining table and roll up my left sleeve.

"Definitely. The Fall flu season is on its way," she says, smiling as she sticks the needle into the inside crease of my elbow. "We should give you an H1N1 shot, too, just to be on the safe side."

"What's that for?"

"Swine flu." Another jab. She makes a note on my card and says, "Your pneumococcal is still good for a few more years."

"Good, because three shots and you're out," I say as I pay her.

"Sloane, always the jokes with you. Now, off you go and stay well," she orders, pointing me to the door.

"Be sure and save some of those condoms for me," I call out a final tease as I head out, tugging my sleeve back down over my elbow.

"You just keep a close eye on your temperature," she shouts loudly after me.

I stop dead. Two steps in front of me in the aisle, looking straight at me, is Himself. He is holding a tiny black and tan beagle puppy in his arms. It squirms and tries to climb up his chest, and finally settles for licking his face as we stare at each other. Then Luke takes a long look at the contents of my basket. My face is on fire. I'm fairly sure he heard the condom crack, and I'm certain he heard Linda's warning. He probably thinks I'm an obsessive-compulsive, hypochondriacal nymphomaniac.

"Expecting a plague?" he says, nodding at the basket.

Where's a deep sinkhole when you need one?

"Or just looking for some attention?" He lifts his chin in the direction of the clinic.

"I *was* injured in the accident, you know – quite seriously. I could have died," I say. Even I can hear the defensive note in my voice. It's cringe-worthy; I don't blame him for sneering.

"The cop at the scene said you walked away with only a few cuts and bruises, not even a broken bone." His eyes flick to my scar.

"Only a few cuts and bruises. Well, that's one way to describe it," I say, thinking of my severed femoral artery, my dislocated knee, my perforated outside and insides, while I watch the puppy chewing on his long fingers.

"So isn't all this a little excessive – even for you?" He gestures with a hand to my shopping and the clinic behind me, while the puppy moves its head to follow the movement of his fingers, trying to catch them with its mouth again. I empathize.

I could try to explain, but what would be the point? I can tell he doesn't want to hear – it would only sound like I'm trying to make excuses.

"I'm a hypochondriac. Just add to the list of my sins, Luke. Write it under H. It comes after G for Guilty and before I for …" I draw a blank. "I for, for … 'ideous."

His mouth twitches, but it may just be a wince because the puppy's needle-like teeth are clamped over the pad of flesh at the base of his thumb. Good, I think savagely, I hope it draws blood.

"Hey, Banjo, take it easy," he says, nuzzling the wriggling puppy's ear.

"Excuse me, but dogs aren't allowed in the store!" A prune-mouthed assistant is glaring at Luke, hands on hips.

Just then, Sienna turns the corner into the aisle. She sees Luke and hurries to my side, glaring up at him like a fierce pixie.

"Are you picking on her again?" She waves a lipstick tube reprovingly at him.

"Been telling tales to get some sympathy?" Luke looks only at me. Then he spins around and heads out.

I discharge some of my anger with a few choice swear words, while Sienna nods and pats me consolingly on the shoulder.

"Idiot! Imbecile!" I say, as we head to the cashier at the front of the store. Oh, right, *now* I can come up with apt words starting with I. Why does my brain never work properly when I'm talking to Luke, only afterwards?

"He is, he really is," says Sienna loyally.

"Ignorant, imperfect, inferior, injured, ill!" It's like I have Tourette's now, too, and can only spit out I-insults.

"Is he?" Sienna asks.

"Is he what?"

"Injured and ill?"

"I'm talking about myself," I say, absently, almost dropping the money I'm trying to hand to the cashier because I'm staring out the storefront to where Luke is playing with the puppy.

He has put it on a lead and let it down onto the sidewalk, and he's chasing the clumsy blur of fur around and around a bench. Then he scoops it up and holds it high up in the air above his head. He's laughing. Luke, I mean, not the puppy – obviously. His face is open with pure joy, his smile is wide. I have never seen him like this, never seen him happy and carefree. A fresh wave of guilt clenches at my throat and heart. This is who he is, or should be. The bitter, angry, hostile Luke that he is with me? That's because of me.

Now he has the pup on its back in the cradle of his arms, and he's gently tickling its fuzzy belly with a look of tenderness on his face. I may be falling in love.

"Insane," I say. "Impossible."

19

Clear and present danger

"Girl, 16, missing after witnessing boyfriend's murder."

Question: Worse?
Answer: Probably.

I imagine what might be happening to the missing girl, amend my answer to 'definitely' and stick the news report on my wall. What will I do when the line reaches the door? Cover this whole wall or double-back and come down the opposite wall? Take the line outside and into the apartment hallway to the elevators?

First thing on Monday, I head for the school faculty lounge because I want a private word with Mrs. Copeman. Students are not allowed inside. Perhaps all their authority would be lost if we discovered what they actually did in there (eat cake and gossip all day, is Sienna's theory), but I get another teacher to call her out for me. It's no big surprise, however, when she refuses to split up the mortal enemy dream-team.

"I'm afraid not, Sloane. I said 'no swapping partners' for good reasons, you know. We can't just change partners when we don't like who we're working with. Part of being in the real world, part of life itself, is having to work with all kinds of people and learning to get along with them. And that's also true of relationships – even marriage!"

"But Luke and I aren't in a relationship, ma'am," I point out. Not in this lifetime.

"The point is, Sloane, we can't just swap partners when the going gets tough."

It's preachy little homilies like this that make students hate L.O., I think, but I don't say it. I didn't want to blub the truth, but I'm getting desperate. I'll try anything now, even the truth.

"But, ma'am, you don't understand," I say. "His brother was killed – last year, in a car accident. Another car crashed into him, killing him instantly. My mother was the driver of that car. Luke's brother died, I survived."

Mrs. Copeman looks shocked and distressed.

"Luke hates me. He can't bear to look at me. There's no way we can work on this project as partners."

Mrs. Copeman studies me for a long time, then she says, "That's hard. I can imagine how that's very difficult for both of you. But there's an opportunity here for you two to work things out. We don't solve problems by ignoring them, or running away from them".

"But, Mrs. Copeman!" I'm pleading now.

"No, Sloane. I'm sorry, but that's my final decision. I suggest that the two of you get together and talk this through, otherwise you're going to struggle with the second part of the assignment."

"We've already done most of both parts," I mumble.

"What are you talking about? I haven't even assigned the second part of the project yet."

"But ... but ... you said there were two parts – the theory and the practical," I protest.

"I said there were two parts to the project, and two sections to the first part," she corrects. "You've still got a whole other part of the project to do, and it will take up much of the rest of the quarter."

I groan.

Question: Can this day get any worse?
Answer: Do vampires suck?

First up is English, with he-who-cannot-be-avoided, L.J., the Perkelator and the gang of girls whom, I have discovered from Sienna, all have names beginning with J: Juliet, Jessica, Jade and – ironically, because she is the plainest – Jane.

"Do you think it's a membership requirement for the clique? To have a J-name," I asked Sienna on Saturday, truly curious.

"Quite possibly. Which means you and I are out of consideration."

"I'm devastated. Heartbroken."

This is actually true, but it has nothing to do with the Jaysters.

Luke is bent over a book on his desk and doesn't look up when I pass him to get to mine, or when I put a note down on his desk. I wrote it earlier so I don't have to speak to him. I'm trying to minimize the amount of direct contact he has to have with me.

L.J. is hulking in his seat at the back of the class, scribbling red lines and geometric patterns across his wrists with a ballpoint pen. He's pressing so hard that I worry he'll tear open the skin. If I had a stick of gum, I'd offer it to him, just to interrupt the scratching. But I don't. So I snag my pocket-pack of anti-bacterial wipes out of my bag, lift the white edge of one wipe temptingly out of the opening and offer it to him. He shakes his head and looks at me like he thinks I'm crazy, but he stops his ink tattoo.

I sit, head in hand, eyes on Luke to see if he's reading my note yet. He's not. The fingers of his right hand are drumming on the desk top, just an inch away from it. Up front, Perkel is writing his word of the day on the board.

"Simile, a noun, from the Latin *similis*, meaning 'alike, resembling'."

Luke's hand suddenly stretches out, snatches the note and opens it. I read along with him in my head.

L

Mrs. Copeman refuses to allow us to swap partners. And there's another part of the project still to go.

Sorry.

S

He crumples the note in his slender hand and lobs the ball of paper into the trash can at the front of the class. He doesn't turn around. I'm relieved. I'm also disappointed because I'd really like to know what the green of his sweater does to his eyes.

Perkel dusts his hands, looks over the students in the class and zones straight in on L.J.

"And what, precisely, is a simile, Mr. Hamel?"

Why does he always address L.J. by his surname? For everyone else he uses their first names. It's like he's *trying* to rile him. L.J. shrugs, looks down at his big hands and fiddles with a hangnail.

"Can you give me an example of a simile? No? Someone else, then – *anyone* else?"

L.J. ignores him. A couple of students have their hands up, but Perkel asks me next. Maybe he's out to press my buttons, too.

"Sloane?"

"Mr. Perkel?"

"Do you know what a simile is?"

"I do."

Somewhere in front of me, someone laughs.

"And yet," says Perkel, looking irked, "your hand is not up."

"That's true."

"Why is your hand not up, Sloane?"

I begin to answer, but apparently the question was rhetorical – he is answering it himself.

"I think that you, Sloane, have adopted the lazy habit of not volunteering in class. Perhaps you do not want to draw attention to yourself. Perhaps you wish to stay, as the colloquial term has it, *under the radar*?"

"Yes, Sloane, you should occasionally stick a hand in the air, otherwise you might go, like, completely unseen and unnoticed." Juliet boggle-eyes my scar while she says this in a mock-kind voice.

"You know, Juliet, when you do that with your eyes, you look even more like a Pekingese pup than usual."

Juliet gasps. I turn to Perkel.

"Was that an example of a simile, Mr. Perkel?"

The class laughs. Juliet seethes. Luke is twirling a pen between his fingers.

Perkel tells us to be quiet and announces, "Today we are doing orals."

The boys snicker at this. I've noticed that there are certain words that always do this to teenage boys. *Oral* is one. *Tongue* is another.

"Unprepared speeches," Perkel clarifies.

We have four minutes to think up something sensible to say on the topic "A clear and present danger" and we are supposed to make notes of what we want to say on the blank pieces of card he hands out. My head is still busy trying to analyze Luke's response to my note when Perkel says, "Time's up!"

True to form, he calls on L.J. first. L.J. shambles up to the front of the class and turns his pallid face to us.

"When you throw a stone into a pond, ripples spread out from the point of impact. Our actions are the same. There are consequences for what we do. For every action, there is an equal but opposite reaction. That's a law of the universe. Actions can be dangerous because of what reactions they cause," he says, then falls silent.

"Is that it? Nothing more to say?" says Perkel.

"I want to quote lyrics of a song, 'Surrender' by Seven Ravens.

Where the waves are still
And the ripples fade,
When the stars burn out
And the devil's paid,
Where the struggle ends in the end of deep,
Sweet surrender there in the silent sleep."

"Why don't you sing it, L.J.ayyyy?" says Jessica. Or perhaps it is Jade.

"Yes, give us a song, Long John," says the other one.

"Larry-Jack, Larry-Jack, Larry-Jack," chants Juliet in an undertone.

"Enough," says Perkel in a tolerant, amused voice. He smooths his pointed beard. "Anything more, Mr. Hamel?"

"Isn't that enough?"

"Not for a decent grade, it isn't."

Perkel waves L.J. back to his seat with a dismissive hand.

"Sloane, you can go next. Don't forget your speech-card."

I walk to the front and turn to face the class. I stare down at the perfectly blank card in my hands, then look around the room, desperately seeking inspiration. Luke is leaning back in his chair, his arms crossed over his chest and his long legs stretched out in front of him. He stares at me, as if waiting to hear – and judge – what I could possibly have to say.

"You may begin," Perkel prompts from his desk behind me.

I have nothing to say. *Clear and present danger.* It sounds like the name of a book, or a movie. Or an accident. The silence stretches out. Perkel clears his throat impatiently.

"Like, anytime now," Juliet calls out. I scowl at her. She is actually brushing her sleek, blonde hair – in a classroom! – with a foul glittery, pink hairbrush. It gives me an idea.

"Few people are aware," I begin, "of the clear and present danger presented by germs."

The Jaysters snicker. Luke shifts in his chair and rolls his eyes.

"Bacteria and viruses lurk on every surface – desks, door handles, stair bannisters and especially on personal items – such as pens," I direct this last at Luke, who is twirling a pen in his fingers again. "And brushes," I say to Juliet. She looks down dubiously at the brush in her hand, puts it down on the desk and then, after a moment, stuffs it into her bag.

"Sick people, diseased people, *infectious* people," I continue dramatically – I'm really getting into this now – "cough and sneeze into their hands and then touch things around them, transferring contagion onto light switches, remote controls, term papers." I emphasize my point with a demonstration. I hack a cough into a cupped hand, then wipe the palm over the corner of Perkel's desk. I'm pleased to see that he is looking discomforted.

"And those are just the polite people. Many people simply cough and sneeze and spit wherever, spewing billions of germs into the air and onto the objects and people around them, contaminating and infecting."

"Gross me out," says one girl sitting in the front, pulling a revolted face.

"Research shows that most people do not wash their hands after they use the toilet. These are the same people who might, minutes later, shake your hand, borrow your phone, or use the ketchup bottle before you in the cafeteria at lunchtime. And that's not to mention the disease pathogens often present in water and raw food, like sushi, under-cooked chicken, and contaminated salad."

The boy sitting across from Luke makes a gagging noise and mimes vomiting, but I'm in my stride, now, and completely confident. If there's one thing I know, it's germs.

"Some of the contagious diseases you can catch in these easily transmissible ways include: influenza, tuberculosis, meningitis, salmonella poisoning, Ebola and Hemorrhagic Fever, and pneumoleucocytic taccycardic osmepsia!"

Okay, so I made that last one up – but it sounded dead impressive. I have the whole class's attention now and, by the expressions on their faces, there will be fewer meals sold in the cafeteria today.

"So in conclusion, I would like to caution you. Before you touch that door handle, consider the herpes viruses which might be lurking there. Before you flush the toilet in the school bathroom, think about whether a person with pink-eye might have touched it before you. Before you kiss that hottie, you may want to check their tonsils for strep-throat. Because unknown, unseen, and invisible though they may be, germs pose a clear and present danger!"

Loud applause salutes the end of my speech, even though some people are wearing expressions which make them look like they just sucked on a lemon. Others are laughing – fake-sneezing and coughing loudly at each other. Luke does not look amused by the raucous reaction of the class. Clearly, no-one is to like anything I do.

"Thank you Sloane, that was most ... informative," Mr. Perkel says. He is looking a bit green about the gills. He likes to dole it out but is not much good, apparently, at taking it.

"Nice one," says L.J. approvingly when I plonk back into my chair. He holds out a hand for a low five and I swipe it. It is soft and damp.

"Germs don't scare me much," he continues softly. "I'd lick your tonsils anytime."

Where did that come from? I make a pained face at him then turn, a little disturbed if I'm honest, to listen to Juliet's speech. It's all about the terrorist threat to the heartland of America. She seems to think that the CIA, NSA and FBI and probably the PTA, too, should spend their time and budgets alternately on bombing the hell out of most Middle East nations and monitoring the phone-calls and email exchanges of private citizens.

I start doodling but look up when Luke's name is called.

"I would like to talk to you all, and to some of you especially," he looks at me, "about the clear and present danger posed by driving while talking or texting on a cell-phone."

I drop my head into my hands and slump onto my desk. This is going to be torture, I think. It is. For the next seven and a half hours, or so it feels, Luke holds forth on the type of negligent, selfish, worthless scum who endanger us all, taking the limbs and lives of innocents, and ruining the happiness of families everywhere. People who drive distracted deserve to die, and those who do not intervene to stop them – who do not forcibly wrangle the phones from out of the driver's murdering mitts – are just as culpable. All the way through, I'm breathing: in for four, hold for four, out for four, hold for four, just as Eileen taught me. It helps me keep the flashbacks at bay, which is good, but it also keeps me in the here-and-now, which is bad, because Luke is still feeding my monster of guilt.

"We've all heard that friends don't let friends drive drunk," he concludes, "but I would argue that passengers who let drivers text and drive, while knowing that this constitutes a clear and present danger, are equally responsible for the murder and mayhem that ensues."

The class is silent after his speech, though Perkel compliments him enthusiastically.

"Well said, Luke! That was an excellent speech on a most important and very relevant subject."

I am crushed, like a car in a compactor, by the stream of bitter agony which Luke has siphoned off onto me. The worst of it is, he's right. I know it. I knew it then – that day in the car, before my life imploded – and I know it now.

Luke glares back at me as the next student gets up to speak. It's a scorching look and I can only stare bleakly back. My cheek is resting in my hand, my whole body is heavy. My head moves – a series of small nods – and I look away, guilty as charged.

20

Cruelty to animals

Luke

I let her have it full-force, so I should feel better.

But I don't.

It felt like kicking a little puppy. A tall, sad, blue-eyed, freckle-nosed little puppy.

21

Resuscitation

It is a law of the universe, observable in high school gym classes everywhere, that girls who spend their summer vacations on the beach in the hungriest of skimpy bikinis will, once back at school, coyly refuse to wear one-piece school swimsuits and get in the water with their male peers.

Of our class today, only four girls, including me, are in the water. The others sit on the poolside stands, talking, checking their phones, playing with their hair, and conspicuously not paying any attention to the boys. The boys strut up and down the edge of the pool, pushing and shoving until they fall into the water, and then attempt to drown each other with savage dunks, all to the accompaniment of loud shouts, taunts and boasts.

I sniff disparagingly at the gratuitous displays of beauty and strength – honestly, it's like some baboon mating ritual – and swim another length, warming up while I wait for the lesson to start. Coach Quinn arrives, spots the posse of passive resisters and walks toward them, as if he intends to challenge them. But whoever he asks will tell him that she has "lady troubles" or that it's her time of the month and he will blush furiously and stammer an apology. Then the other girls will look at him with wide, wounded eyes and berate him for his male insensitivity, before surrounding the girl and escorting her off to the locker rooms, where, I know, all of them will have a good laugh and some of them will have a smoke. Coach halts halfway to the girls, thinks a moment, then retreats to the safety of the males of the species.

The best part of swimming for me now, A.S. (I realize I haven't thought this term for a while), is the pleasure of submerging my face in the water and feeling that my body is still strong and functional as I cut through the water. I'm not as powerful or fast as I used to be, but I could still beat most of the boys here. Even though I can feel the click in my knee and the pull in my thigh, I push myself until my muscles burn.

I have forgotten my goggles and cap, and my eyes sting from the chlorine in the water. The Shrink says forgetfulness and short-term memory impairment is a symptom of post-traumatic stress. At our last session, she also told me that I have a "sense of foreshortened future". She says I'll battle with thinking and planning for the long-term future because, having come so close to snuffing it, I struggle to conceive of a future in which

I live to a ripe old age. All I know is, I feel old already as I hang onto the side of the pool, trying to catch my breath.

Luke is in my Gym class – the gods are without mercy – but happily, the Jaysters aren't. Sienna usually is, but she's off sick today with the flu. I have an in-built heat-detecting radar inside of me, and it tracks the hotness that is Luke to where he stands with the boys – who have no biological excuse to get them out of exercise. I clutch the wall, looking at his swimmer's build: broad shoulders tapering down to a slim waist and flat stomach. His muscles are long and lean, his skin tanned and free of blemish.

I turn my back when a boy dive-bombs into a nearby lane, sending a deluge of water my way. Coach blows his whistle to get everyone's attention and says that today we are to practice life-saving. We've already done the theory – today it's time to get practical. True to his usual sexist way, he appears to believe that only girls can drown and only boys can save. It's not like I need the practice – I have my advanced certificate in life-saving – but I still resent the assumption. There are ten boys, but only six mannequins, so the coach calls out to the girls in the pool.

"You, ladies! Act like you're drowning."

Two of the girls, one in a red latex cap and the other in a blue, immediately start screaming in mock panic, raising their arms in the air as if to summon the boys. Two immediately respond to the call and strike out to the flailing giggling girls. I have a premonition of dread.

I cross my fingers and keep my back turned to the boys' side of the pool.

"You, Ben, pair up with that girl over there, in the black cap," he says.

Behind me, someone groans a complaint. Magda – the girl in the black cap – is in the lane next to me, treading water. She is overweight and unpopular and apparently no guy's first choice for a damsel in distress.

"At least she'll float easily," someone whispers.

There is a tightening of Magda's mouth, but otherwise she does a passable job of pretending she never heard the comment.

I know what is about to happen. The skin on the back of my neck prickles and it is not from the drips of cold water that fall from my hair, which is pulled into an untidy knot at the top of my head. I turn to the sound of loud splashes. Coach is shoving the life-saving mannequin torsos into the pool with kicks of his feet. They look like the bald, expressionless, androgynous remains of a shark feast, as if a great white had chomped through them, biting off both arms above the elbow and everything below the waist. Mad thoughts crowd my mind. Is this so they don't have to make mannequins with genitals? Or do we only need to know how to save torsos? I hang onto the wall-edging as I wait for what I know is coming.

"You," says coach, pointing at one of the figures in the water who hasn't yet snagged a mannequin, "you can save her – the one with the … uh … no cap."

I know what he was about to say, and I know who he has just spoken to. There is a moment of silence among the boys. Apparently, while it is considered acceptable to poke fun at fatties in the water, it crosses some line to mock the facially disfigured. Or maybe it is my demeanor that gives them pause: I turn to face them and stare a challenge, and no one dares a smart comment. Still, they give Luke commiserative pats on the shoulder as he swims out to where I am.

"Bring the victim to the surface and then tow them to the far wall using the cross-chest tow I showed you last week."

I lift my arms into the air, exhale deeply and sink down into the deep water. Luke dives down and swims into position right behind me. He wraps an arm around my waist, fingers splayed across my ribs. My skin burns with awareness where he touches me. He tightens his grip, then tugs me up to the surface. On the trip up through the blueness, we bump into each other and my body registers every point where we touch. I gasp a breath as we break the surface. He brings his left arm over my left shoulder, across the top of my chest and tucks his hand under my right armpit. It is warm against the coolness of my skin and even though my face is out of the water, I cannot breathe. He pulls me onto my back and heads backwards for the far side of the pool, kicking and sculling water with his free hand. I am, to all intents and purposes, lying on top of him. I know he must be hating this contact. I stiffen and start to freak out, not knowing how to endure the knowledge of the revulsion he must be feeling.

"Just relax," he says into my ear. "Pretend you're unconscious."

I force myself to relax, muscle by muscle. How is it possible that we haven't reached the other side yet? Part of me wishes we never will. It feels so good to rest against him; I wish he could just save me from all of my life.

We reach the wall and I clamber out quickly, so that he doesn't have to touch me again. We sit on the paved surround, saying nothing, waiting while the others drag their partners and mannequins to the pool's edge and out of the water.

"This is when you might need to do CPR – Cardio Pulmonary Resuscitation. Watch while I demonstrate the ABC's and remember what I taught you. You ladies over there, come over and watch please," says coach and he takes us through the whole process, showing us the techniques on the orange mannequin which lie limbless and inert in front of him.

"Now it's your turn to practice on your partners."

Oh, for the love of fudge! There is an eruption of giggling from red cap and blue cap, Magda looks like her worst nightmare has come true, and Luke curses under his breath.

Aloud, he says, "Are you kidding me?"

"You're obviously not really going to do proper compressions or breaths on the live girls, you boys who have partners, but you can practice the movements."

I lie down on my back, wishing I were truly unconscious. It's cool out of the water and I am covered in goose bumps; I'm desperate to cross my arms over my chest where, I'm sure, the evidence of my chill will be obvious to Luke.

"A is for airway, so check for obstructions to breathing," shouts coach above the excited hubbub.

I open my mouth reluctantly and Luke peers into it like a buyer inspecting a horse's teeth before the sale. He does not stick a finger into my mouth as the other boys are doing with their mannequins, for which small mercy I am grateful.

"B is for breathing," shouts coach. "See if you can feel the warmth of their breath against the palm of your hand, look closely to see if their chest is rising or falling."

Red and blue cap's partners respond to this very enthusiastically – examining their victims' chests closely like myopic diamond-inspectors – and there is a fresh outbreak of irritating giggles and ribald comments.

"Coach!" yells one boy as he prods his lifeless mannequin. "I think I'm man-down over here. It's not breathing."

I'm woman-down over here. I can't breathe either. Heat radiates from Luke's hand as it hovers over my lips, his ear almost touches my chest as he listens for breath and my fingers itch to wrap themselves into the wet hair at the back of his head. How can my heart beat so hard, thud so violently beneath my ribs when I am not breathing?

"C – start compressions! You four with the real girls – just pretend, please. We don't want any cracked ribs. But I need to check you've got the position right – heels on the sternum, two fingers off the end of the bone – and the right rhythm with your arms."

"Woohoo," says the boy crouched above the girl in the red cap. He rubs his hands together, then stretches them out and prepares to lay them on her chest.

My eyes are wide open – perhaps I am dead, rather than unconscious – and they are drawn irresistibly to meet Luke's. He looks at me, his expression fathomless. I am sure mine is not. I draw a ragged breath and stare at him for an endless moment. Then his hands, so big, so warm, move so that one is above the other, fingers intertwined where I wish mine were. He places the heel of the bottom one down, gently, just touching on the skin above my sternum. His fingers are carefully pulled upward so that they don't touch the curves which rise on either side of the bone. Still, we look at each other.

"Uh-uh-uh-uh-staying-alive, staying-alive," the old Bee Gees hit blasts out from the music system, beating out the speed and rhythm we're supposed to use for compressions.

"Faster, you lot. Do it in time to the music," shouts coach. "Thirty compressions, then two breaths into the mouth. Don't forget to pinch the nostrils closed."

There is a lot of laughing, cheering and singing around us, but it is somehow distant, apart from the immediate reality that is us. My world has narrowed to this moment, to Luke and me.

Luke pulses out the compressions, absorbing each push in his bent elbows, rather than pushing down on my chest. I count the pulses. My heart has never beat so vitally, so quickly, as when he approaches thirty. Then he lifts his hands and brings his face over mine. He can't mean to ...

I stop breathing again. There are flecks of gold and shards of emerald in the green of his eyes as they come closer. Drops of water cling to the tips of his black eyelashes. His lips hover over mine, almost, but not quite, touching and I can't help what happens next. My lips part and they rise up to close the minute distance, and then they are touching his. His lips are dry, warm and surprisingly soft for a mouth usually set in such a hard, grim line. My heart kicks somewhere in the pit of my belly as his lips begin to return the pressure.

"Enough! Enough! You kids!" says coach disgustedly.

We pull apart immediately, not looking at each other, but coach is staring down at the girl with the red cap and her partner who have abandoned any pretense of pulmonary resuscitation. Their lips are locked together and they are kissing each other passionately, while all around, classmates hoot and cheer. The girl is still wearing her goggles and I notice that they are steamed up. I steal a glance at Luke, but he leaps to his feet and walks to the concrete steps where towels are scattered in colored heaps, snatching up one and wrapping it around his waist, rubbing another over his face and chest.

My heart still races as I sit up and try to calm my breathing. I look for a towel in which to hide my flushed face. My lips tingle, my breath is ragged. I feel more alive than I have in months – in over a year, if I am honest. I have been numb, going through the motions of my life. Today's CPR was effective. I might not have been dead, but I realize that for the longest time, I have not been truly alive.

22

Frozen

Luke

The last twenty-four hours have been craptastic, and I figure things are about to get worse. Might as well get it over with.

Mom or dad?

Mom is in the living room, gazing with unseeing eyes at the TV where a documentary on Antarctic wildlife is showing. Dad is on his computer in the study. I know he hates to be disturbed when he's working and I don't think I could handle another lecture about the importance of his job given the strained finances of our family. So ... Mom, then.

I'm about to hand her the letter when I see that her eyes are brimming with tears. I'm guessing it's not the whales on the screen who have set her off. She's lost inside herself again.

I give her shoulder a soft squeeze and head to the study instead.

"Hey, dad?" He looks up when I place the envelope on the desk beside his keyboard. "You need to read this and sign it."

"What's this?" he says, extracting the letter. Even before he begins reading, he's frowning.

Banjo runs in and leaps up against my legs, demanding to be picked up. Dad's scowl deepens at her yelps.

"Can't you keep her in the kitchen?"

"No."

Neither of my parents is happy about the new addition to our family. Dad says dogs are expensive and where will we find the money for her food and vet bills. Mom hasn't said anything directly, but she flinches at the noise and motion, and steers clear of engaging with my puppy. I don't understand how this is even possible, because Banjo is the cutest, sweetest, softest creature there ever was. She melted my heart the first time I saw her. But maybe mom's is more frozen, like one of those icebergs she's watching.

I'm ignoring their negative reaction to Banjo. Saving her is the best thing I've done all year. I'm beyond bummed out that I can't save them all. Last night I wanted to adopt all the doomed animals from the shelter, but no way would my parents have allowed me to bring home two dogs and three cats. So all I could do was go with each animal into the procedures room and hold them while they got sent into the sleep that they would never wake from.

On the way home, it all just felt too heavy to hold inside. I wanted to cry. I wanted to break something or hit someone. I did not want to have to make dinner and watch while mom didn't eat it and listen while dad described his last game of golf.

I was still feeling really down this morning when Sloane came in the classroom, rubbing hand-sanitizer between her palms and fingers. What is *with* her? Her hair was still wet from swimming, and that reminded me irresistibly of what I've been trying to push out of my mind for the last few weeks. Images from that damn gym class flashed through my mind – her impossibly long legs, the feel of her body against mine in the water, how her swimsuit clung to her curves, the way her lips moved to touch mine, the way my body reacted.

Argh! It feels like a betrayal of Andrew to remember that, to think about her in that way. This is the daughter of my sworn enemy. I had her on the floor under my hands. I should have strangled her and yet I almost kissed her. What is with *me*?

Then Perkel arrived and started his usual BS again, playing favorites and acting like a total asshole. Who the hell asked him to hold me up as some kind of example to the world? Then I got hit with a bunch of flak about being the pretty boy with all the looks and talent and money (ha!) and lucky breaks. It's ironic really, because "golden boy" was never *my* role. It would've been funny, except that then all hell exploded and now here I am standing in front of my frowning father, waiting for the inevitable.

Annnnnddd, here it comes. Dad looks up from the letter, gives a deep sigh and says, "This is very upsetting, Luke. I can't think what's got into you." Really? *Really?* "We never had problems like this with Andrew. I'm sorry to say that I'm very disappointed in you."

Yeah, take a number, dad.

23

Fire fighting

I am sitting in the small waiting area outside Principal Comb-Over's office. Miss Kazinsky, his secretary, has explained that he is running late.

"Mr. Como is meeting with the parents of a student on a very urgent matter," she says, breathy with excitement and running her hand over her bouffant, brassy-red hair. They have seriously bad hair in the admin block of the school. Como earned his nickname from the long, dark strands of hair carefully combed over and affixed to his balding skull. Opinions vary as to what he might use to hold it in place: spit, axel grease and Miss Kazinsky's lip gloss are some of the less revolting guesses.

"You'll just have to be patient for your appointment, I'm afraid," she says.

I can be patient. With ease and with pleasure, I can be patient. As I sit here, staring at a copy of The

Desiderata which is stuck to the wall opposite me, I am missing L.O. I consider it a lucky escape. For the past few weeks, Luke and I have been working as separately as possible on part two of our project. When we've had to work together, he has been business-like and impeccably polite. When we work apart, he pays me no attention. At least he has stopped glaring at me. Except for how my body registers his presence, his absence and his every move, it's like the burning hope and horror of the Gym class never happened. Coach Quinn has declared our class "too immature" to learn responsible life-saving, so we're back to practicing softball throws and catches in the gymnasium.

I have tried to focus on my own life, catching up on work where I am behind, reading our assigned English text (*Atonement* by Ian McEwan), spending time out with Sienna, practicing my photography and trying to make new friends. I have been making a real effort *not* to focus on Luke. It's a bit like trying not to think of a pink elephant but, still, I was doing a reasonable job. Until yesterday.

Due to a serious lack of motivation, I'd cut my before-school swimming session short, so I was a little early for English class. The room was empty as I walked inside, except for Luke, who was busy with a folded piece of paper at the windowsill on the far side of the room. Curious, I edged over to take a look. Luke was, very gently, easing a spider onto a piece of paper. Moving slowly and carefully, he brought the paper up to an open window and gave it a little shake to release the critter.

He turned, gave me a long look, then swallowed and said, "What?"

"Rescuing a spider? Really? You couldn't just swat it?"

"There's too much death in the world already," he said, which effectively put me in my place – in the naughty chair in the guilty corner.

The other students arrived in twos and threes. When L.J. shuffled in, alone, some of the kids razzed on him, which set the Jaysters to singing the lumberjack song again, sending a twitch rippling across L.J.'s shoulders.

"Shut up. Just get off his case," I told both groups of smart mouths.

"Ooooh," said Juliet, shaking her blonde hair, "the monster puts her foot down!"

"Oh grow up."

L.J. took out his sketchpad and drew something in black ballpoint on the paper – a man with hollow eyes, bleeding gums, outstretched arms and intestines spilling from a vertical slash up his stomach. I think it was a zombie, though I'd be the first to admit that I am no expert on the undead. He must have been unsatisfied with the picture, because he crumpled it up and swept it to the floor. I craned my neck to read the title scrawled at the top: *Lifeless Jerk.*

Everyone was in their seats or sitting on the tops of desks, chatting and checking phones, by the time

Perkel arrived – ten minutes late – and called the class to order.

"Forgive my tardiness. I was meeting with Principal Como. That reminds me, Sloane, your transfer documentation is apparently still outstanding, plus Mr. Como wants a quick chat with you. You are to take your personal file and all completed transfer forms to the Principal by no later than tomorrow. He says to set up an appointment – Miss Kazinsky keeps his diary."

We were spared the word of the day ritual; Perkel hurried straight on to the day's assignment.

"This is an exercise in personal, private writing. You are to write down three lists of goals for yourself – short, medium and long-term goals. Where would you like to be, what would you like to have achieved at the end of the next six months, the next year, and the next five years?"

There was the usual round of questions as the class tried to delay beginning the work – if we could only blow off another twenty-five minutes, we would have wasted the whole lesson – but Perkel soon shut the queries down.

"No, Mike, it is not too difficult. I am not asking you for a doctoral thesis in post-modernism, just a list of goals. You can do this. You have only ten minutes to complete the exercise, so get cracking, please."

Fifteen minutes later, Perkel read out L.J.'s goal. (He has only one, apparently.)

"Goal for the next six months: to become a zombie killer. A zombie, or Homo Coprophagus

Somnambulus," Perkel sneered the words, "is one of the walking undead, a person with no soul, personality or imagination, who goes through the motions of life, destroying and feeding on living humans to satisfy their unnatural appetites."

Perkel shook his head, as if saddened by the words.

"What am I to do with you, L.J.? Do you have no real goals for your future? Failing to plan is planning to fail, my boy."

Get off his case, already, asshat!

Let's see someone else's work, shall we?" said Perkel.

To no-one's surprise, he moved to Luke's desk and picked up Himself's list. I sat up straight in my desk and leaned forward, eager to hear.

"That's private, Mr. Perkel," said Luke.

Nooooo. It was the perfect time for Perkel to be an insensitive, tactless ratfink so, of course, he came over all considerate and respectful.

"Of course, of course. But I do not think I am betraying confidences –"

(There were *confidences* in Luke's list? I had to get my hot little hands on that paper!)

"– when I commend you for setting goals for your sporting achievements,"

(Ha! Sectional or National swim team, I bet.)

"academic achievements,"

(Yes, yes, get on with it!)

"family life –"

(He set goals for his family life? Weird. I wondered what –)

"and charitable community involvement."

Wow. Luke did charitable community work. I resolved at once to end my slothful, boob-tube watching ways and to volunteer at the local homeless shelter or orphanage. Eileen was right – I have been over-involved in myself. If I knew where Luke volunteered, then I could offer my services there, too. No, no, no. I had to stop thinking like that.

I would have given my right arm to read Luke's list. Okay, not literally, but I really, really, *really* wanted to see it. A lot. My own list looked a little shabby by comparison:

Get over myself.

Get over Himself.

Make some goals for my future.

Yup, one of my goals was to make some goals. Perkel was rabbiting on again. I tuned in when I heard him say Luke's name.

"You know, you could take a leaf out of Luke's book, L.J."

"Yeah, yeah – he's got the looks, he's got the talent, he's got the family, the big bucks, the shiny future and all the breaks."

Luke turned to face L.J. He looked like he wanted to say something, but L.J. wasn't finished.

"I've heard it all before, I don't need to hear it again." L.J. sounded angrier than I had ever heard him before. "Pretty boy's got the goods, alright."

This was unfair. Sure, Luke had looks and talent, but he had bad stuff to deal with, too. We all did.

"What did you call me?" Luke asked L.J., his voice low and flat.

L.J. ignored him and spoke to Perkel instead.

"He's a real eligible bachelor, is pretty boy. So, have you popped the question yet? Eager for the wedding night?"

"Just what are you implying?" Perkel demanded, his face pale and livid, at the same time as Luke stood up, toppling his chair over backwards, and strode right up to L.J.

"Say what you have to say to my face, L.J."

"How dare you? How dare you!" spluttered Perkel. "You rude, ignorant little –"

As suddenly as if a button had been pressed on a detonator, L.J. exploded. He lifted his desk into the air and tossed it to the front of the classroom. It flew over the heads of several students, who yelped and ducked, spilling paper and pens and crashed against the board. Then L.J. lumbered forwards to tower over Perkel.

"No!" he bellowed. "How dare *you*? You are rude, you are ignorant and *you* are little."

He held his chunky thumb and forefinger about two inches apart in front of Perkel's horrified gaze.

"And I've had enough of you." L.J. poked Perkel in the chest with a finger, then gestured to the whole class with a sweep of his arm. "Of all of you! And specially of you, pretty boy." He flicked Luke's hair.

"Don't touch me!" said Luke, slapping L.J.'s hand away.

L.J. stretched out a hand and shoved Luke's shoulder. "Bring it on, pretty boy."

"Boys!" Mr Perkel shouted, but neither of them paid any attention to him.

Luke and L.J. were circling each other now, in the small space at the front of the class. I was nervous. Luke was as tall as L.J., but L.J. was bigger, meatier, heavier – no question.

Perkel's high-pitched protests were lost in the babble of excited voices. A group of boys chanted, "Fight, fight, fight!" while everyone formed a circle around the pair, shoving back desks to make more space. A few, including me, climbed up onto chairs to get a better view. L.J. shuffled around in a circle, as heavy and clumsy on his feet as a grizzly bear on hind legs, his huge paws held up in front of him, while Luke bounced and weaved on his toes. L.J. shot out a meaty fist directly at Luke's face, but Luke pulled back and ducked the blow, before shooting out an up-and-under fist. It clocked L.J. square on the cheek. Around me, there were groans and gasps. I couldn't utter a sound – I had half my hand stuffed in my mouth.

L.J. shook his head and staggered, but didn't fall. Several students cheered and shouted bloodthirsty encouragement.

"Let me through, let me THROUGH!" Perkel yelled, pushing his way through the throng and fumbling with the big red fire extinguisher grasped in his hands. He pointed it at the two wrestling figures now locked in some kind of slowly rotating Sumo death grip, then sprayed them with the white foam, aiming most of it – or so it seemed to me – at L.J., and hitting him with a direct blast into the face.

L.J. turned, fists raised, and blundered toward the rapidly retreating Perkel. When he pulled back his arm for the punch, Luke grabbed it from the back and pinned it behind L.J.'s shoulder, then wrestled him backwards, away from Perkel. Two other boys joined in to restrain L.J., who was yelling wild threats at everyone.

Perkel, flushed and breathless, smoothed his beard and thanked Luke repeatedly for intervening, but I strongly suspected that Luke didn't do it on the teacher's behalf. The male of the species can be strange sometimes.

"I heard they're calling L.J.'s parents in," Sienna told me later in the day. "He'll be suspended for sure, maybe even expelled. He's lucky Luke stopped him from getting at Perkel, else he would have been charged with assault. Luke has just been given a letter of warning to take home – his parents have to sign it. But he won't get suspended because Perkel told Comb-Over that he was provoked."

"How do you know all this?" I asked.

"I have spies everywhere," she said darkly.

24

Private papers

I'm jolted out of my thoughts of yesterday's drama when the door of the principal's office suddenly opens and L.J. comes out. His must be the parents in the urgent meeting with Como.

"Just wait out there while I have a final word with your parents, L.J.," calls the principal from inside the office.

L.J. leaves the door open a crack and Miss Kazinsky doesn't get up to close it – perhaps she is hoping to hear some juicy tidbits. Everyone knows that she is a flaming gossip, and Sienna says she couldn't fill half the pages of Underground West Lake without this prized informant.

L.J. slumps heavily into the chair right next to me. It creaks.

"So, how did it go?" I ask.

"I'm suspended for a week. Like *that's* supposed to be a punishment." L.J. shrugs.

I don't know what to say to that. Voices coming from the office intrude into the silence.

"The boy is a little wild, sir, but I'll lick him into shape. It comes from never having a stable, male authority figure in his life. He didn't know his real father. His mother never really settled down, did you, Lila? And there has been a passing parade of men, only two of whom married her. So the boy's life has been unstable, and it shows – I don't deny that. But I'm Lila's husband now, and that's how things are going to stay."

I stare down at the manila folder in my hands, acting like I can't hear the loud, clear voice and pretending to read the forms inside – my transfer documentation, medical reports and transcripts of academic records.

"I'll be expecting a clear improvement in behavior when he returns to school." That must be Como speaking.

"Yes, sir. I'll teach him a lesson when we get home, don't you worry about that. He needs to grow up and be a real man. I'll make sure he understands the importance of self-control."

"Well, I wouldn't want you to be overly harsh with L.J." Como sounds worried now.

"Nothing like that, I assure you, sir. But 'Spare the rod, spoil the child' I always say. Thank you for your time, Principal. Lila, you thank Mr. Como now, we need to be off."

A man steps out of the office. He is short but compactly built, with a trimmed moustache and buzz-cut hair. Behind him trails a thin woman, wearing a loose shirt, a fringed cotton skirt and flat leather sandals. Long grey hair falls around her face as she smiles in a distracted way at L.J., and fiddles with the necklace of gemstones and crystals around her neck. Mr. Como, his hand hovering behind the small of her back, escorts her out of his office.

The man stands rigidly, as if at attention, glowering at L.J.

"Goodbye," says Como, shaking their hands and ushering them out. "Just wait here for me, L.J. Miss Kazinsky, give me a few minutes to complete the paperwork on the meeting. I'll give you a buzz when I'm ready for you to send this young man in."

Wiping his face with a handkerchief, the principal retires to his office.

"Are those your parents?" I ask, trying to maintain the fiction of ignorance to spare L.J. embarrassment.

"I'm not related to *him*." He picks at a scab on the back of a knuckle.

"Hey, L.J.?"

"What?"

"I'm sorry... About everything, you know."

He turns to face me. I wish he wasn't sitting so close. I feel sorry for L.J. – even more so now that I've caught a glimpse of what things are like for him at home – but I don't much like him in my personal space.

"You know what I'd like?" I continue. "I'd like for people to back off and stop bullying and leave you be."

Uh-oh. At once I can tell I've put my foot in it. There's a look in his eyes as he studies me that tells me I shouldn't have said this – or anything. I should just have let it be.

"You know what I'd like?" he says.

I shake my head.

"I'd like to lick your scar and see if it tastes the same as the rest of you. We could have some fuuunnn, you and me."

He sticks his tongue out and waggles it. The pink, fleshy moistness is pierced with a silver stud. I can't help myself – I shudder, try to cover my instinctive reaction in outrage.

"Why do you *do* that? Why do you always do that?"

"What – salivate? Lick people?"

"Why do you always push people away by being revolting. Do you like being alone?"

"Like I would be Mr. Popular if I just played nice," he mocks. "Like it matters what I'm like on the inside."

Now I feel guilty, because he's right. No-one even knows, let alone cares, what he's like on the inside. Not that he lets anyone get close enough to know him. It looks to me like he goes all-out to keep people at a distance. Maybe it hurts less that way.

"Nobody in this place can see past the ugly. *You* know what I'm talking about." He reaches out a finger to poke my scar, but I slap his hand away.

"You make it hard, L.J., you make it so hard."

"I'd be easy for you, baby."

Ugh!

"Stop it!" I snap. "Cut it out."

"What? It's not like any other guys are lining up to get their hands on you, Scarface."

Miss Kazinsky's buzzer sounds and she orders L.J. into the office. Her eyes are on me. I feel flushed and hot – am I just bothered, or do I have a fever? I'm feeling my forehead, as a mother would her child's, when I look up and see Himself standing in the doorway, watching me. I whip my hand away and squint at the poem on the wall, trying to read the first line. *Go placidly amidst the noise and haste, and remember what peace there may be in silence.* Indeed.

How long has he been standing there?

"I have an appointment with Mr. Como," Luke tells Miss Kazinsky.

"Take a seat, Mr. Naughton. He's running late. Your appointment is after Miss Munster's."

Luke is holding a white envelope – it must be the letter he had to get his parents to sign – and he passes it restlessly between his hands.

The uncomfortable silence lasts eons. By now, I must be missing art class, too. Miss Kazinsky leaves and returns a few minutes later with two mugs of coffee, just as L.J. and Como emerge from the office. L.J. walks out.

"Who's next?" the principal asks his secretary as she hands him one of the mugs.

"Sloane Munster – the new transfer from Lincoln High. Then Mr. Naughton, the other party in the Hamel altercation."

L.J., who is standing in the hallway just outside the door where Como can't see him, flips Luke the bird.

"I'll buzz when I'm ready," says Como, without a glance at me. He heads back into his den, blowing on the hot coffee.

As soon as Como's back is turned, L.J. leers at me and licks his lips suggestively before ambling off down the hallway.

Irritated and upset, I stand abruptly, forgetting the folder of loose papers on my lap. It spills to the floor and the sheets flutter through the air, glide across the polished wooden floor, and come to rest under the chairs and the low central table.

"Monkey nuggets!"

I get down on my hands and knees to collect them into a pile. Luke gets up to help, but I stop him.

"Don't bother, please."

He settles back into his chair while I grub about on the floor trying to gather up the papers without getting them too dirty. I think I have them all and am sorting them back into a semblance of order inside the file cover when Luke speaks.

"What's a partial splenectomy?"

My head snaps up. He has a piece of paper in one hand. Even from six feet away, I can tell it's the summary of my medical records – and he has been reading it.

"Nothing. Give me that!"

I try to snatch it back from him, but he lifts it high above his head. I'm tall, but Luke is taller and there's no way I can reach it.

"What's a partial splenectomy?" he repeats.

"What are your goals?" I counter.

"What?" he says, thrown. His hand lowers slightly in surprise, but when I make a lunge for it, he pulls it back up again.

"The goals you wrote down in English yesterday and wouldn't let Perkel read out," I clarify. "What are they?"

He shakes his head, grinning.

"Those are private," he says, staring down at me. His eyes are more green than brown today.

"So are my medical records."

"Answer the question, Sloane."

"*You* answer the question!"

"I asked first."

"What are you – nine?"

By now I'm hopping up and down, trying to get the form. I feel ridiculous. I turn when a buzzer sounds. Miss Kazinsky is staring at us with avid curiosity.

"You can go on in now, Miss Munster. Give her the paper, Mr. Naughton."

I grab it as soon as I can reach it. Our hands touch and this time, I notice, he doesn't flinch.

I stuff the form into the file and march stiffly into Como's office. While he studies the paperwork, I stare out of the window which overlooks the visitor's parking lot. A man has a big boy pushed up against the side of an old, battered pickup, one hand thrust against his chest, holding him in place, while the other wags a pointing finger under the boy's nose. A woman in a long skirt stands a few paces back, looking down at the ground, where her sandaled foot traces a pattern in the gravel.

25

Mission impossible

"Right," says Sienna, tucking her corkscrew curls behind her tiny, pixie ears. "This evening, your mission, should you choose to accept it ..." She interrupts herself to hum the theme from *Mission Impossible*.

We're at the school pool, watching the first swim meet of the season from the concrete steps at the side. West Lake is facing its two arch-rivals – Cordoza High and Wheeler High – and the competition is fierce. There's a lot of screaming and shouting echoing off the high roof and brick walls. We don't officially have cheerleaders for this sport, but that hasn't stopped the Jaysters from donning matching short red skirts and skimpy midriff tops, and waving red and white pompoms.

Luke is swimming in this race – Varsity boys' freestyle, 200m. My body longs to be in the water, racing – especially when I watch our girls team. I'm better than they are – or I used to be. My mother was certain that one day she'd see me at the Olympics, clutching a medal.

"Go for gold, Sloane, aim high," she always said.

Did her advice apply to boys, too? I suddenly miss her fiercely.

"Your mission," Sienna says again, snapping her fingers in front of me. My eyes must have glazed over.

"Right. My mission?" I duck to the side to avoid a shower of water that sprays up as the closest swimmer hits the water.

"Your mission is to photograph the five or six hottest hunks and most bodacious babes on the swim team. What we need, though, is a close up of the face and a separate body shot – each guy's torso, each girl's booty."

I raise my eyebrows. "What's it for?"

"For The Underground. I thought we could jumble up the head and body shots and have a competition to see who could match them up correctly. The winner gets bragging rights and a candy bar."

"You don't think that's objectifying their bodies?"

"Don't overthink this, agent, it's just a bit of fun. Also, we'll be doing it to both males and females, so it's not like it's sexist."

"Yes!" I say. Luke has just won the race.

"You'll do it, right?"

"You want me to run around taking pictures of the girls' backsides, and the guys' abs?"

"It's a tough assignment, but someone's got to do it."

Sienna and I look down at the pool where the swimmers are just emerging from their racing lanes. Water streams off their long, lean muscles and flies off in droplets as they pull off their caps and shake their heads like wet spaniels.

We both sigh. Actually, I sigh twice – I'm looking at Luke.

"So how's it going with him?" Sienna asks.

"Who?"

"Sloane, please," she chides. "You're talking to me."

"Fine. It's going ... not too bad, I suppose. We're working separately as far as possible on the L.O. project, and he's not giving me such a hard time."

We both look at the winners' podium, where Luke now stands on the middle block, dipping his head for the medal.

"He *is* ... gorgeous," says Sienna, rolling the word around in her mouth like a juicy grape.

We both nod, then sigh again.

"He has to be one of the hunks in the competition, for sure," she says, suddenly all business.

"Sienna, no way! No way can I go up to Luke and ask him to bare his body –"

"Just his abs," Sienna says, mock horrified.

"– to bare his abs so I can take a photo of him."

"Do it on the sly then," she suggests. "Pretend you're a photojournalist spying behind enemy lines."

I must still look unconvinced, because she punches me on the arm and says in a hearty, encouraging voice, "Sometimes we have to suffer in pursuit of our art, Sloane. Just do it. Take one for the team."

"Why can't you do it? What are you going to be busy with that I have to slink about, stalking the swim team?"

"I'll be taking some informal shots, and," she says, reaching into the enormous bag she carries everywhere and extracting a giant tube of Pringles, "pumping an informant for info."

"You're going to bribe a stoolpigeon with chips?"

"Not bribe, Sloane, never bribe! Boy, you sure are cynical. It's simply that she is going to dish the dirt, and I am going to gift her with a snack."

Sienna is what my mother would have called 'incorrigible".

"Later, girl friend," she says.

I catch the faint strains of the spy tune again as she hops downs the stairs and heads towards the exit. I can just make out the brassy red hair of the person waiting for her in the shadows there.

I grab my camera and make my way down to where the swimmers are milling about waiting for races or toweling off after them. The bootylicious girls are only too eager to pose, though they keep wriggling and giggling, and insist on removing their caps and combing their hair before they'll allow me to shoot their faces. Still, photographing the girls is easy compared to the boys. It's damned embarrassing to ask the muscled male swimmers to strut their stuff. A couple look as embarrassed as I feel, but most are shameless – volunteering to go full-frontal in the buff while sucking in their stomachs and clenching their muscles to make their six-packs pop. One guy, who has "Eat my bubbles!" written on his back, rolls up his latex swimming cap and stuffs it into his speedo before posing.

After I've got head and torso pics of all but one of the male contenders, it's time for the money shot. I cannot make myself approach Luke directly. I creep about, hiding behind the winners' podium and the score-keeper's table trying to get the photographs of Luke, but he is either in constant motion or surrounded by a bevy of smiling girls. I take cover behind a bulky man standing on the paved pool deck and raise my camera. I'm after Luke's torso. He is some way away and he has a towel slung around his hips so it's not ideal, but this swim meet will soon be over so I figure I'd better take whatever shot I can get. Also, my feet are getting wet because I'm standing in a puddle of water.

I aim and focus carefully. My finger is just pressing the button when, through the lens of my camera, I see him walking directly towards me. I pull the camera down. This is when I notice that my shelter has waddled off and I'm exposed. There's no point in hiding the camera – he's already seen it – so I just stand like a dope in a puddle as a half-naked Luke approaches me by the side of the pool, and am overcome by a horrible sense of déjà vu.

"Are you stalking me?" he says, and I'm relieved that he doesn't look angry.

"No! Yes. Sort of. I have to get shots of the swim team. Faces and ... torsos." Heat floods my face – I either have scarlet fever, or I'm blushing big time.

"You want a photo of my torso?"

"It was Sienna's idea – she insisted," I say quickly. "For her blog."

"Sure," he says and when I make no move, asks, "Do you want to do it now?"

"Do it? Now?"

"Take the photo, I mean." Is it possible that he's blushing now?

"Oh, right."

I quickly take a shot of his face. Too quickly – the small onscreen display shows me it's blurred.

"Sorry."

I fumble with the settings and take another shot. Then a few more – just to cover my bases for the assignment, of course. Now it's time for the body shot.

"This okay?" says Luke, striking a pose with his hands on his hips.

"Can you ... um," I wave a hand at his towel, too mortified to say the words.

"Strip?" he asks, raising an eyebrow.

I hide behind the camera while Luke removes the towel. I only hope that the steam inside me comes out my ears, not my mouth – I don't want to fog up the viewfinder. I take the shots, slowly and carefully, as befits a person respectful of her craft. Below his chest

– broad and smooth and tanned – are the lean muscles of his six-pack. Actually, it looks like a ten-pack to me, but I have no time to count now. I'll have to make an enlargement later and study it at home. *Stop it! Focus!* I chide my wayward mind. A dark line of hair leads down from his navel to his speedo. *Enough.*

"Got it, great, thanks," I say. I wish I had something to fan my burning face.

"No problem."

He wraps the towel around his hips again. We stare at each other for a long moment, then look away at the same time as the pack of swimmers passes us. Senior girls, 50m fly.

"Do you miss it?" he asks.

"Yeah," I nod. "I miss a lot of things."

"I found out what a splenectomy is – I searched it on the internet. Why did you have to have your spleen removed?"

"Only about half of it, they were able to save the rest."

"Why?" he repeats.

"It ruptured. In the accident."

I can't believe we're talking about this. That I said the A-word. He places a warm hand on my arm above my elbow, and my heart stutters. But then he moves me gently to the side and I see it's to allow some people to pass by. My arm feels cold, kind of exposed, when he removes his hand.

"It sounds rough," he says.

"It's not too bad."

"Is that why you take all the pills and vitamins, and why you're obsessed with germs?"

"Yeah. Your spleen is like the home of the immune system. When it's removed, you're more susceptible to infections and complications. So you have to be careful."

"And a titanium pin in your knee."

"I'm a real Frankenstein's monster."

"And a severed femoral artery."

"It could've been worse," I say and immediately want to kick myself. Of course it could have been worse – who knows that better than Andrew Naughton's brother? But Luke doesn't take the opportunity to twist the knife.

"Yeah," he merely says, "but it's a little more than 'only a few cuts and bruises'. Look, I'm sorry I gave you such a hard time. I was a real –"

"Don't worry about it, really. There's nothing you need to apologize for. It's no more than I deserve."

"But you –"

"So," I interrupt, changing the subject. "I did some digging on you too – fair is fair. If you read my private records, I should get to read your private goals."

"Oh yes?" Am I imagining it, or does he look concerned? "How did you do that?"

"Google. I entered the search string: 'What are Luke Naughton's short and medium-term goals'."

"Of course. Any results?"

"Only 38,977," I boast. "Do you know that you're the karaoke king of Kansas, a hockey player for the

Pittsburgh Penguins, and the author of a book entitled *Turkey Farming for Pleasure and Profit*? Ooh, and you're wanted in three states for public indecency."

He throws back his head and laughs. It's that joyous carefree laugh I saw when he was holding the puppy. If I had a tail, I'd be wagging it now.

"Funny," he says. He reaches out a finger and touches the tip of my nose. "Funny one," he says again and, still grinning, he strolls away to the starting blocks.

That night, in the quietness before sleep, I realize a whole day has gone by without my thinking of my mom. Guilt sits on my chest, heavy as a marble gravestone. "The length of your pain is not a measure of the depth of your love" – I repeat Eileen's words over and over to myself. But I still feel like a bad daughter, and the tears are as much for my guilt as my grief.

26

Blissed out

Sienna and I are walking past the lockers after school ends for the day, comparing homework woes, when Luke falls into step alongside me.

"Hi," he says.

"Hi," I respond. Brilliantly.

"I'm needed somewhere else – urgently," says Sienna, and she melts away to join a group of friends.

"So," says Luke.

"So," say I.

"Are you mocking me?"

"Would I dare?"

"So … I was thinking."

I want to prompt him for more, but my brain reminds me that I had the cafeteria special for lunch today – vegetarian lasagna – and I'm overcome with the worry that there is spinach on my teeth and garlic on my breath. I keep my mouth closed.

"About what you said about fair's fair."

"Yeah?" The word slips out as I turn my face to look at him. I close my mouth again.

"I did read your entire medical record – you could say I know you from the inside out," he says, with a quick grin.

"More about the 'fair's fair' part, please," I say.

"Well, I wondered if you wanted to see me busy achieving one of my goals?"

"Yes, I'd like that." Am I hallucinating? Is this actually happening?

"I'll pick you up at your place – 4p.m. okay?"

"Today?"

"Sure – is that a problem?"

"No, no problem."

He looks me up and down from head to toe, frowns at my dress and low-heeled sandals.

"Wear your oldest clothes. And sneakers," he says and then disappears into the throng of students heading out.

Sienna materializes back into the spot next to me and demands a word-for-word action-replay of the last two minutes.

"Old clothes," she muses. "*Old* clothes?"

I nod.

"Not a date then," she concludes.

"I hardly think Luke Naughton wants to ask me out on a date," I say.

"Oh, I don't know. He can't seem to stay away from you."

"He's probably going to drag me out into the woods somewhere, chop off my head and fingertips, and bury the remains in the damp earth," I say, remembering this morning's newspaper article.

By a quarter to four, I'm dressed in faded and fraying jeans, an old but warm sweatshirt and purple canvas sneakers, ready for either my outing or my ending. My aunt drops by to check on me and it's all I can do to get her out of my apartment by the top of the hour.

"My partner on a school project is coming by to collect me," I say. "We have to go take more pictures of pollution."

I grab my camera and wave it around as evidence.

"You're going out dressed like that?"

Aunt Beryl never looks this casual – even when the triplets have flung food and toys and each other at her.

"We're going to some mucky places," I explain.

"Just be sure that you and she don't go to any sketchy or dangerous places, Sloane – safety first!"

"Safety first!" I chime, steering her towards the door. "Give a hug – or three – to Devon and Keagan and Teagan."

The buzzer sounds from downstairs just as I close the door behind her. I press the button on the intercom and tell him I'll be there in a minute. I grab my jacket, bag and camera, and fly down the stairs.

Luke drives an old-fashioned, sky-blue VW beetle with silver trim. He folds his long limbs into the low seat, and with a roar of the loud engine, we set off.

"This is one cool car," I say.

He eyes me as if to check whether I'm being sarcastic or not.

"Really, I love it," I say.

It's true – something about it makes me want to smile. I feel like I'm in a toy car as I peep out of the windscreen, and twiddle the old-fashioned knobs and dials on the blue metal dashboard. The radio still works – though it's stuck on a golden-oldies station – the wipers wipe and there's an image of a fox on a castle in the center of the steering wheel.

"Want to press the horn?" he asks as we pull up to a set of lights.

"How did you know?"

I lean over and toot a tune. This prompts some discourteous hand signals from the driver in the car in front of us, and we both laugh. I'd do anything to keep him laughing.

"Where are we going?" I ask.

"You'll see."

We bounce along down the road to the sound of the sixties and, too soon, we pull into the parking lot alongside a long, low building. The sign outside reads: *West Lake Animal Sanctuary.*

"You volunteer at an animal shelter? That's your community service goal?" I guess.

"I do."

I should have known – the way he plays with puppies and saves spiders.

"You're okay with dogs and cats? Not afraid?" he asks.

I make a dismissive noise to indicate that I have no fears of our furry friends. Then I'm struck by a thought.

"But if there are pet rats and mice – you can have them all to yourself."

"Don't like rodents?"

"They have no bladder control. They dribble wherever they run on their creepy little paws."

"That's actually a myth put out by pest control services," says Luke. "But they do pee a lot, and some like to mark their territory."

"I'll stick to Fido and Whiskers," I insist.

The animal shelter has a front office where everyone greets Luke by name and they give me a friendly welcome when he introduces me. Then, armed with rubber gloves, buckets, liquid soap and scrubbing brushes, we head out back to where the animals are housed. The day is cool, winter will be here in a month, but at least the sun is shining.

"We're cleaning cages today," says Luke. I have a feeling, from the way he checks to see how I react, that this is some kind of test.

"Point me in the right direction and tell me what to do," I say enthusiastically, but I'm checking him out, too. I don't know whether he brought me here to spend time with me or to sentence me to hard labor for my crimes. I guess the latter might be the more likely scenario when he hands me a purple plastic spade and some paper bags, and sets me on poop-scooping duty in the cat cages. The cats eye me disdainfully as I clean their litter trays, holding my breath against the gag-worthy smells.

By contrast, complete pandemonium breaks out when Luke walks down the lane that runs between the rows of cages. Dogs bark, hounds bay, puppies whine hysterically and they all hurl themselves in friendly welcome at the wire. Even the cats deign to amble up to the front of the cages so he can give them a welcoming tickle.

It's heartbreaking – and not just because I wish his fingers were touching me. There are dozens of animals, all rescued or abandoned, locked into simple cages with a shelter at the back and a small square of concrete at the front. The animals look fairly healthy, but some of the older ones have obviously had a hard life. A couple of the dogs limp, one has only three legs, and there's a mean-looking marmalade-colored cat with only one eye and half an ear missing. A small pot-bellied pig, by the name of Christmas, and several rabbits snuffle about in the last cage of this row.

Suddenly Luke is at the door to the cage where I'm busy.

"I'm sorry – I forgot about your immunity thing. You probably shouldn't be near cat litter."

"It's fine," I say, waving my hands in their bright yellow rubber gloves. "Anyway, this is the last one."

"Here," says Luke, when I've dumped the revolting contents of the cat litter trays into a large bin labeled

"Poop". He tucks the nozzle end of a hosepipe into my hands – I've been promoted!

"You can spray the floors of the dog cages. Try to angle it so that the water and mess runs into those gullies along the side of the cages, rather than into the shelters at the back of them, where their bedding is."

"Shouldn't we get them out first?"

"Nah, the ones that don't like it will hide out at the back, but some of them will enjoy the shower."

They do – some dogs stand right under the spray and a few try to bite the stream of water, barking madly and running around in circles. By now I'm sweating in my jacket, so I enjoy the fine cool mist spraying off the water which the breeze blows my way. Meanwhile Luke carries an old dog out of his cage and walks over to a deep stainless steel sink. He lowers the dog gently into the warm water and lathers him up with the foamy soap.

"Can't he walk?" I call over the sound of the hose and the hounds.

"He can, but he's stiff with arthritis, aren't you old man? And he loves baths."

The dog does seem to be wearing a contented smile under his grey muzzle.

"Are all these dogs and cats waiting for adoption?"

"Yeah, they have to be sterilized before they can be adopted, though. It's the shelter's policy that no pet goes out and has more unwanted babies. And money is tight, so they don't get to save as many lives as they could. There's a shortage of space, and food costs plenty, so they can't afford to keep an animal for longer than six months."

"What happens to those that don't get adopted in time?" I ask, although I can guess.

He winces.

"They have to euthanize them. It breaks my heart. But there's no real option otherwise. Some of them are rescued from inhumane owners and conditions – they can't go back. And if they run feral on the streets, that's no good either. They work really hard here to find good homes – advertise in the paper and on their website. Tyrone Carter – from our L.O. class? – he set up their website for them, and helps them run it."

"I'm impressed – with the both of you."

"It's little enough. I just wish we could do more. I want to study veterinary science, so this means a lot to me."

I'm ashamed. I have had my head stuck so deeply up my own ass for so long it's a disgrace. My scar pales into insignificance beside this magnitude of need, and my past losses are less pressing when set against the immediate demands of the here-and-now. I need to start thinking about the future, about doing something worthwhile or meaningful. I can still make my mother proud – I believe that.

"Can I help?"

"Can you hold onto Moses for me while I fetch a towel? I'll want to get him out as soon as I've rinsed this shampoo off him. Don't let go or he'll try to jump out."

"Sure," I say, turning off the hose and walking over to keep the mutt steady in the sink. "But I meant can I help in some way with the shelter – in general, I mean?"

I rub the shampoo lather through Moses' coat. He likes the massage, pushing up against my hands as if urging me to reach a deep itch, but he sneezes in disgust when he bites a large soapy bubble.

"For real?"

Luke reaches up to where the towels are piled on a high shelf and my eyes stray to the narrow band of skin exposed between his shirt and his jeans.

"Sure," I say, dragging my eyes away. "I'd like to help."

"They can always use more volunteers – to help with work like this," he says, pulling down a stack of towels. "Or else you could donate food or blankets, or sponsor a sterilization."

"I'm in."

I'm so distracted by his slow smile as he returns (I swear there's a hint of approval in those eyes!), that my hands stop moving and I forget to hold onto Moses. The mutt braces his legs and shakes his body violently, spraying Luke and me with dirty dog water and splodges of foam.

On the way home, we turn the Beetle's ancient heater up to full blast, letting the warm air blow over our damp clothes and teasing each other about who smells worse.

"No, it's you – definitely," he says, touching the back of my hand with a finger. I want to flip my hand over and lace my fingers tightly through his, but he needs his hand to shift gears.

"Oh yeah, how do you figure that?"

"Smell is subjective, right? And relative, too. And relative to what girls are supposed to smell like, you smell worse. Guys are supposed to smell sort of … real."

I surrender to the logic of this and lean my head back against the seat, alternately gazing out the window at the world, and at Luke's hand on the gearshift. I am totally blissed out.

27

Surrender

Luke

I've been a dick. That's the thought that occurs to me before I fall asleep. I, Luke Naughton, have been a judgy dick.

I've given Sloane a hard time not because of anything she did, but because of whose daughter she is. Which is way unfair, because none of it was Sloane's fault. She wasn't the one texting and driving. Her hands weren't the ones on the steering wheel.

And, anyway, what gives me the right to judge anyone? Nobody's perfect, especially me. Bottom-line? It was an accident. A freaking tragic accident.

Mrs. Copeman has a bunch of inspirational posters on the walls in her class. In small print, at the bottom of the *Forgive* one, it says, "When you forgive, it doesn't mean you condone or approve. It means you put down the resentment and bitterness you've been holding onto. It means you let go of the hope that the past can be different."

All this time, I thought it was my anger and hatred that was keeping me going. But really, it's been keeping me stuck. Am I ready to move on, if that means I have to forgive Sloane's mother?

I don't know. I don't know what Andrew would want me to do. I only know that I want to be with Sloane, that I want to get to know her better.

Christmas and Moses have given her their approval. Maybe it's time I did, too. Because here's the thing: I really like her. A lot. She's brave, and generous and compassionate, and she makes me laugh. She's different to the other girls at school. She seems more mature – I guess because she's been through so much. And yet she's not so hung up on looking cool that she's afraid to get dirty or have fun.

Also, she's H-O-T.

I've been fighting this thing between us, but I don't want to fight any more. I want to surrender.

28

Smitten

I can be crafty when I need to be. In between hosing cages and poop-scooping at the animal shelter, I casually wangled out of Luke the times when he regularly volunteers and, over the next two weeks, I schedule my volunteer sessions to coincide with his. It's not that I'm not really there for the animals, it's just that menial labor is much more pleasant when I'm able to do it in Luke's company.

We chat easily and share jokes, and classes with him at school are fun now, too. But I'm beginning to despair of it ever going any further. Only Christmas, the potbellied pig, shows any affection for me. If only I could charm my way into Luke's heart with some sugar cubes and dog treats.

Just when I'm getting desperate enough to ask *him* out on a date, a move which Sienna assures me is against "the rules" and should not, under any circumstances, be contemplated, Luke suggests we catch a movie. I'm quicker to agree than Christmas is to sniff treats out of my pockets, which is saying something.

Luke takes me to a movie festival at the local independent cinema and we watch some crazily complicated thriller with dreams and spies and plenty of shoot-em-up car chases. And fights where characters climb the walls and ceilings – literally. Perhaps Luke is checking out my intelligence. If so, then I'm snookered because about half an hour into the film, just as my arm is developing a cramp from where I've cannily left it lying on the arm-rest for easy access, Luke takes my hand. He holds it and plays idly with my fingers, then he strokes a finger down the palm of my hand and my brain disengages entirely. I stare at the screen, like a movie-goer is supposed to, but all my attention is on my hand. And his. My fingers actually tingle at the tips.

Within minutes, I no longer have a clue what's going on in the movie, so when Luke asks me afterwards whether I think the top stopped spinning at the end, I have to fudge it.

"That's the real question, isn't it?"

"Yeah," he looks intense. This film is a favorite of his – he told me he's seen it seven times. "Was it real or just a projection of his desires?"

"Mmm."

"But what do you think?"

"Umm … I think it could play out either way, we can never know," I spin it like a politician.

"Yeah, there's just no resolution to the uncertainty, to what's real and what's not. That's deep."

I must be shallow. The biggest question revolving in my head is if he ever intends to kiss me. Not tonight, he doesn't – is the answer to that question. He drops me off outside my apartment building, making no move to kiss me. I'm about to make the first move – the wrath of the dating pixie be damned – when his phone sounds an alert. It's a text from his mother. He says she's not well and he needs to get home. Dang it.

Luke waits until I'm safely inside the glass security doors before driving off with a wave and a toot of the Beetle's horn. I'm so full of crackling, frustrated energy that I choose to run up the three flights of stairs instead of taking the elevator. It occurs to me, somewhere between floors, that the reason he didn't ask to come upstairs might be that he doesn't want to see the picture of my mother again. It's the photo we used at the funeral service. I had it enlarged and framed, and her name and the dates of her birth and death are printed at the bottom in gold lettering, so it's a vivid reminder of the accident, and that, after all, still hangs between us, unspoken and carefully ignored.

"Or perhaps," I suggest to Sienna in art class the next day, "he's playing hard to get. If so, it's working."

"That's supposed to be your role!"

"This is a play and we're acting?"

She sighs at me; I am not a good dating protégée.

"The girl is supposed to be cool and aloof and hard to get, Sloane, everyone knows that! Well, everyone except you, apparently. You've got to make him work for it."

"Can't," I say hopelessly. "I'm smitten."

"Smitten?!"

"Smited, smoot, smote. I am, as the Perkelator would say, enamored."

"Ooh, girl, you got it bad."

No kidding. I'm so besotted that I've stopped printing out horror-stories from the news sites. I find myself tempted to cover my apartment wall in pictures of puppies and rainbow unicorns and moonlit lakes instead. All of the pictures I took of Luke in the swim meet are now also on my cell phone, where I stare at them on a regular basis. If I'm not careful, I'll be practicing a new signature next. I'm counting my chickens before they hatch. I'm nuts. And I'm in denial about the reality of the past which hovers just behind and between us. We have never actually spoken about the accident in any kind of detail; it's as if there is some sort of unspoken agreement between us never to mention it again.

"How about we grab something to eat tomorrow night?" Luke asks in Thursday's English lesson.

"Sounds good, but it's my treat."

When he protests, I insist. When I tell her about it later, the dating pixie gives me a lecture on the status of male-female relations. Evidently, little has changed since the Middle Ages.

"You're supposed to let the man pay," Sienna says, shaking her head at my waywardness.

"If he always pays, I'll bankrupt him."

"If you pay, it'll emasculate him!"

"Not possible," I say, and lose myself in a pleasant mental stock-take of his various masculine qualities.

It takes a judiciously-aimed eraser to jolt me out of my daydreams.

"Ow!"

"Where are you taking him?" demands Sienna.

"I thought that little Mexican Cantina near my place?"

Sienna approves; she nods. "More importantly, what are you wearing?"

That's a question I still haven't answered twenty minutes before I'm due to meet Luke at the restaurant. I've tried on half-a-dozen outfits, even though I strongly suspect that unless you're baring mega cleavage and leg, guys couldn't care less what a girl wears. I settle on jeans and a blue, button-up shirt, hoping it brings out the color of my eyes. I put on some mascara, blush and lip gloss and glower at my scar, which makes all the primping relatively pointless. Then I loosen two more buttons on my shirt – distraction seems to be my battle plan – before shrugging on a jacket and running the two blocks to the restaurant.

Luke is already waiting when I arrive. We head in together, and the staff greet me and take us to a good table in a quiet corner.

"They know you here?"

"I used to come here often – before. With my mother – she never had much time for cooking dinner."

I shouldn't have mentioned my mother, I should have kept it light. But the mariachi music and the brightly colored tablecloths and the faded piñata hanging in the corner have brought vivid memories of her back to me.

I risk a glance at Luke. He looks back, not smiling, not frowning. What is he thinking?

"And I think I keep them in business with all my take-out orders." Keep it flowing, girl, I can almost hear Sienna urging me.

Diversionary tactics are called for. I take off my jacket, his eyes drift to the display, linger for a long moment, then travel quickly back to his menu.

"So tell me, what's good?" he asks, and we're off, over the awkward moment.

When the rotund waiter arrives to take our order, I ask for tacos, medium heat, with an extra side of guacamole. Luke asks for chicken chimichangas – hot.

"Is señor certain?" asks the waiter. "Eez very hot."

"Is very very hot," I confirm.

"I like it hot," says Luke.

"I bring you a big jug of lemonade. And a big jug of water." The waiter takes our menus and disappears.

"He's not kidding about it being hot," I warn. "Even the *medium* here is plenty hot enough for me."

"That's because you are not the Chili King – I am," says Luke earnestly.

The waiter brings our lemonade, two frosted glasses, corn chips and salsa for starters, and a small bowl of minced jalapeño chilies to go with our main meal.

"The Chili King?"

"Yes, the undisputed King of chili. Do not let it upset you, querida. Take heart from the fact that you are in the company of royalty."

He speaks in a formal way, with a half-Spanish half-Mexican accent which sets me giggling, and I melt a little at the endearment. But I cannot ignore the challenge.

"You are sadly mistaken, señor."

"Que?"

"You may be the king, but I am the Chili Queen, and it is a foolish peon who does not acknowledge that the female of the species is more deadly."

"Perhaps," he suggests, twirling an imaginary moustache, "we should settle the matter in a duel?"

"But of course. I accept your challenge. It will be as nothing to me."

With a flourish, I move the bowls of corn chips and minced chilies to the center of the table. I select a large, curved chip, scoop up a bite of green jalapeño and, in front of his amazed eyes, pop it into my mouth.

My tongue screams a protest. Flames scorch my throat. My eyes water. I want to gasp and pour the jug of lemonade straight down my throat, but I force myself to dare him by raising a disparaging eyebrow before I pour myself a glass of the cool liquid and attempt to sip it in a ladylike fashion.

"I am the Chili Queen. You concede defeat?" Although the air moving down my throat is its own kind of torture, I am pleasantly surprised that my voice still works.

"Never! I shall never surrender. But I am delighted to have found a worthy opponent." Luke scoops up a larger portion of the evil green fire. "To your health, and mine," he says, lifting the chip in a toast before eating it with every semblance of pleasure.

"There is perspiration on your brow, hombre," I tell him.

"You, too, are sweating, querida."

I *am* sweating. Like a pig – a real hog, not a sample swine like Christmas.

But I state haughtily, "You are mistaken, señor. Horses sweat, and gentlemen perspire. But ladies merely glow."

"You glow most beautifully."

Wait, did he just say I was beautiful?

"Let us fan the fire of your glow," he laughs, pushes the bowls closer to me and I repeat the self-inflicted torture.

We take it in turns to insult and show up the other – it's like a drinking game, only we're getting high on pain-induced endorphins rather than alcohol – and the chilies are finished by the time our food arrives and we agree to an honorable tie.

We chat about school and friends and swimming and movies. I give him a brief account of my father, then we steer clear of further discussion of family. There is no mention of the big A. And while we talk about PC technology and find out that we both hate Facebook, we do not talk about cell phones.

I find out that the three things he hates most in the world are dishonesty, cruelty and cheating. We discover that neither of us likes limiting ourselves to favorites (colors, music, food), and neither of us likes Perkel.

"I can't stand it when he takes on L.J., especially when he compares us," he says.

"I hate that, too."

"It was great that you stood up to him that time – 'comparisons are odious'. That's really true. No-one should be made to feel second-best compared to someone else." He says this fervently, like it's personal.

I excuse myself to go to the restroom – all that lemonade! – and pay the bill en route. In the restroom, I check my teeth for food while I wash my hands with anti-bacterial soap from a tube I carry around, and reapply my lip-gloss sparingly. My eyes are bright and my cheeks flushed. Maybe chilies *can* make you drunk.

Outside the early evening light has turned the greenish-yellow of an impending storm. The sky is bruised with heavy clouds, and there's the smell of rain in the air. Luke drives me home as lightning cracks the sky but, this time, he gets out and opens my door for me. We stand outside the circle of bright light at the entrance to the building. He holds both my hands and looks deeply into my eyes, as if searching for the answer to some vital question there. I'm lost in those eyes, falling, drowning.

My heart is in manic-depressive mode, lurching forward in a rapid rhythm and then stopping altogether as he cradles my face in his hands. I lean into him.

He tilts my face upwards, then lowers his mouth and finally – finally! – I am kissing Luke Naughton.

29

Storm

I wrap my hands behind his neck, twist my fingers into his hair, melt into the hands that pull me tight against the heat of him.

Luke's kiss tastes of lime and salt and hope. It makes my bones melt, my fingers tingle and my head dizzy. It starts an ache in the pit of my belly and a plea in my heart.

Please, I want to say, *please, please, please.*

But I have no breath to speak and, when he lifts his head from mine, neither has he. We stare at each other for an endless moment.

Please. Am I begging him, or God, or fate?

A sudden deluge of rain breaks the spell, drenching us and driving us inside. We pick up where we left off on the elevator ride up, and the kiss continues in my apartment – first up against the news wall, then on the sofa. The storm streaks the sky with veins of white and pelts the window with rain as we touch each other, running our hands over hair and under clothes, blindly exploring angles and curves, hollows and swells, rough and smooth, hard and soft.

"Wait, stop. Time-out." I come up for air, gasping.

I would love nothing more than to sink back into the delirium, but if I don't hit the brakes, this is going to wind up where it's headed, and I'm nowhere near ready for that. He looks as stunned as I feel. He runs his fingers through his hair. I give a shaky laugh.

"Coffee?"

He nods and I go to the kitchen to make it. My legs still feel weak – I never realized until now that 'weak at the knees' is a literal description – and my hands tremble as I make the drinks.

We sip for a while in silence, pressed up against each other on the sofa. He studies the photograph of my mother on the shelf opposite. I should probably offer to move it to where he isn't confronted by it.

"Luke –" I begin, just as he says, "Sloane –"

"You first," I say.

"I've been thinking a lot lately, about you. And your mom, and the accident."

My heart kicks, but it's not the delicious race that was the pounding rhythm of our kisses. It's unpleasant and frantic; suddenly, I'm scared. It's all too good to last.

"For a long time, I've been bitter and twisted up into knots from the loss of my brother. He was a great guy, you know? Everybody loved him. He was bright and kind and funny. Just the best."

"He sounds kinda … perfect."

"Maybe I'm idealizing him. He could be an irritating know-it-all, and he couldn't catch or hit a ball to save his life. But he was a genius, a real one – he got accepted to Harvard pre-med, with a great financial assistance package thrown in … He was everything I'm not."

Something clicks in my mind.

"Not_A – your online name, is that what it means? Not Andrew?"

"Yeah, I was feeling kinda sour and sarcastic when I made the name up. He was special, and so good that you felt bad to envy him. My folks were so proud of him – he was their golden boy, you know? When he died, they seemed to lose … their way. So did I. We all gave up in some way. But I've learned something from you: we can't choose what happens to us, but we can choose how we respond. What happened to me, to my parents, was not our choice. But who we've become since, is."

"Luke –"

"Hang on, I'm trying to say something important here. I'm trying to say that we Naughtons don't have exclusive rights to grief and misery. You lost a lot, too. Your mother, and your swimming. And you were badly injured – I know you've suffered. But you didn't give up, you're trying to move on. You keep living and fighting – that takes courage. I admire that. I admire you."

He takes my hand, squeezes it.

"I'm not the only one who has suffered – that's what I've realized. And it's time to let go of what was, and deal with what *is* – now, in the present. He's not coming back – I've got to accept that. And I've got to accept what your mother did, and know that she didn't do it on purpose. I'm ready to forgive her, Sloane."

But is he ready to forgive me? I need to know.

"And what about –" I begin to ask, but he's not finished.

"It was an accident. That's the long and the short of it – it was an accident. Yeah, she was on the cell and she should *not* have been. That was wrong. But if she'd just gone straight, she wouldn't have hit Andrew. Your mom swerved to avoid those kids and there wasn't time to swerve again to miss him. In a weird kind of way, my brother took a bullet for those kids. He saved their lives. Huh, just like him to be the hero."

"But ... but..."

Doesn't he know? A black hole of terror and loss is opening up behind me. Just a few words will push me into it, but I have to speak them.

"Luke, in the accident, it wasn't really her – my mother, I mean – who swerved ..."

"Yeah, I know – it wasn't a conscious decision, it's like your instinct and reflexes take over. Like another part of her was behind the wheel."

He doesn't know. I just assumed he knew the details. Knew that I am the one who was indirectly responsible for Andrew's death. I thought that he was growing to like me in spite of it. But he doesn't even know. And if this is how angry and bitter he's been with me when he thought my mother was to blame, how will he be when I tell him that my hands were the last ones on the wheel? I'm going to lose him. The panic rises inside, a hot red tide.

"Luke, I need to tell you something. Something important." My heart is in my throat now, I can hardly speak past it.

"Me too. Me first." He looks at me and his eyes are intense and full of tenderness and a peace I've never seen in them before. "I'm falling for you, Sloane. I'm falling deep and fast."

He kisses me then and God forgive me but with his mouth on mine and his hands tangled in my hair, I cannot find the words or the courage or the will to tell him the truth. I have to tell him, I know I must. But I don't.

I can't bring myself to kill the joy that transforms his face, or the happiness that has transformed my life. Until just a few months ago, it felt like I had lost everything: my mother, my talent, my future, my health, my beauty, my hope, and any sense of feeling truly alive. I can't survive losing him, too. Not when I've just woken up from the deadness and the pain.

He leaves when the storm ends outside; inside of me it continues unabated.

30

Heaven and hell

I'm in heaven.

And I'm in hell.

Heaven is going out with Luke. (It's official now.) Heaven is sitting in the couples' loveseat at the cinema, watching him watching a movie. Heaven is going for long walks in the park beside the lake and having a pizza picnic in the last of the Fall sun. It's waking up on a Saturday and knowing I'll be spending most of the next two days with him. It's the smile of delight that lights up his face when he first sees me in the morning, and the lingering last kiss when we say goodnight. Heaven is talking for hours and holding hands and staring at his beautiful eyes whenever I want to. And it's his hugs, which make me feel safe and calm and wanted, like I've come home.

Hell is the guilt which termites holes into my happiness, and which cripples my hope with fear. Hell is holding onto the secret which has the power to destroy my heaven. It's the deceit and the hidden and the unsaid which holds me back from completely letting go. Hell is the terror of knowing that I will lose him if I'm ever brave and honorable enough to tell the truth, and it's knowing that unless I'm brave and honorable, I'm not worthy of him.

I'm a coward. I'm still clear on what I should do, and I still can't bring myself to do it, especially now that I know how he feels about deceit and cheating.

And it is a kind of cheating – not telling Luke the truth. I'm betraying him into liking, maybe even loving, someone he would hate if he knew the whole truth about her. I know what I must do, but the heaven is so good and the hell of losing him would be so bad, that I do not confess. I concentrate instead on life at school, and my aunt Beryl, and Sienna's blog, and anything else that will distract me. It's easier to focus on someone else's problems or bad behavior than my own.

L.J. is back at school and Perkel wastes no time getting on his case, picking on him to answer questions in class, checking his (and only his) homework on a daily basis, keeping up a steady barrage of snide comments, and reading L.J.'s every English exercise aloud to the class. I don't think L.J. writes too badly at all, actually, even though his essays and poems are filled with zombies and violence, and something he calls the "bliss of non-being". But Perkel reads them in such a sarcastic and belittling tone that they wind up sounding moronic.

L.J. is still a walking contradiction. One moment he's unexpectedly thoughtful or kind, and the next he's being repulsive again. The other day, for example, he saw me walking down the hallway to Miss Ling's room, struggling to keep all my art supplies balanced in my arms, and he offered to help me carry them. He even opened the door of the classroom so I didn't have to touch the handle. But when I thanked him, he said, "I can think of much better ways you can thank me, Munster." When I told him to shut up, he laughed and said he was just kidding, but I wasn't sure. I can't read him and that makes me feel off-balance around him.

I'm worried about him, though. At lunch yesterday, I saw him intently reading something on the cafeteria notice-board. I checked what was posted there on my way out. Unless L.J. is planning on auditioning for the school's new acapella singing group, or has lost a pair of jazz shoes, or wants to volunteer as a mascot for the upcoming basketball tournament, then he was reading a poster about teen suicide prevention.

The Jaysters still haven't given up their quest to discover L.J.'s real name though, for a while, they are completely distracted by the mind-blowing reality of Luke and I hooking up.

"Her?" Juliet exclaims loudly in perfect range of my hearing when Jane tells her the news. "Luke Naughton is dating her – the scar monster? I don't believe it!"

"She must be putting out big-time. What else could the attraction be?" says Jayweedledee.

"Yeah," says Jayweedledum. "I bet they spend a lot of time in bed at night. He can't see her face in the dark."

Juliet glares at me whenever she sees me. When she is confronted with the evidence of Luke and me sitting together in the cafeteria at lunch, or holding hands and sneaking kisses in the hallway between classes, she comes up with a new theory.

"It's pity – that's all it is. He feels sorry for her. Luke's all about community service and helping the less privileged and taking care of ugly dogs. She's an ugly bitch, too. She's just, like, his latest project."

I suspect that a lot of other people probably think the same thing. Luke is hot property, and he's out of my league, no question. Hell, it's a mystery to *me* why he likes me. The more time I spend with him, the more I discover how wonderful he is. He's strong and talented and admirable. He's a truly good person: kind and thoughtful and generous. He's also smart and funny, despite his theory that only his brother possessed those qualities. And, of course, he's so gorgeous he makes my eyes water.

He's doing well in his swimming, too; he's qualified for sectionals and is determined to make the national team. I go to all his swim meets, watching and cheering from the stands. Sienna often keeps me company, bringing her laptop and updating the Underground online news while I watch the heats. She chides me for not submitting more photographs to the gallery, but between homework, dating Luke and helping out at the shelter, I don't have much time. Suddenly, my life is full to the brim.

I've confided in Sienna about Luke's misunderstanding and my perfidy. I was half hoping she would advise me to keep the secret, but she only said, "Stop drowning in guilt and fear. Guilt demands confession and then paying your debts or making amends. And the only cure for fear is action. You've got to do what you've got to do – and only you know what that is."

I forced myself to tell The Shrink, but she won't tell me what to do either, though she points out that both 'fessing up and staying silent come with positive and negative consequences.

"I can't make up your mind for you, Sloane, but I will say this: lasting relationships are built on mutual respect and honesty."

She asks me every session if I've decided what to do yet. It makes me feel worse, so I've cancelled the last two sessions with her. Eileen would say I'm avoiding and evading. Eileen would be correct.

At least Sienna doesn't nag me, but this might be because she's been too busy worrying about the security on her website after a recent incident when someone tried to hack into it.

"Though why anyone would want to, I've no idea," she complains to me crossly. "It's not like I've got celebrity sex videos or credit card information stored on the site. You would think that they'd rather try to hack the school system – upgrade their academic records or something!"

"You think it's someone from the school, then?"

"Who else would give a rat's rotten rear about Underground West Lake?"

The pixie has not been in the best of moods lately. She's been out on a few dates with a student from the local college where she's taking an advanced course in digital photography, but I gather it's not going well.

"I don't know that I'm ready for college boys – they want it all and they want it now," she grumbles.

There's a flurry of dating happening lately: Luke and me, Sienna and her pushy college-boy; Miss Kazinsky and (if rumors are to be believed) Coach Quinn; and Juliet and the geeky Tyrone Carter. I'm cynical about the motives behind this last unlikely hook-up. Tyrone's status and hallway cred have risen markedly – he gazes adoringly at Juliet, visibly delighted and amazed at his good fortune in landing one of the hot babes. Juliet mostly looks at Luke. If she's doing this to make him jealous, she's wasting her time. He is as unaware of the coy glances she throws his way as he is of the cuddles she smothers Tyrone in every time Luke is in the vicinity.

Back at home, all three of the triplets have a cold, which is keeping my aunt conveniently out of my business. I help her out by doing some grocery shopping for her, but she trusts no one to take care of the boys when they're sick, so I'm off the hook when it comes to baby-sitting. I haven't told her about Luke. Partly this is because it's all so unbelievably bizarre – "Yes, thanks, I'd like another piece of pie, Aunt Beryl, and oh, by the way, I'm dating the brother of the boy who died along with mom in the car crash," – and partly it's out of a superstitious dread. If I say it out loud, if I tell anyone (apart from Sienna, who is an exception due to her pixie magic) that I'm in love with Luke, or even dating him, I'll jinx it.

I've taken to finding, printing and sticking up awful news stories again. (First I had to straighten and repair the line of articles – our passionate hallway-kissing ripped a few pages off the wall.) The obsession had faded for a while, but now it's back with a vengeance, and a twist. Before, I used to measure the degree of badness against my injuries and past losses, but now I measure it against my guilt and deceit and dreaded future losses. I stick up the latest report: "Mass shooting in cinema kills 12, injures 50".

"Worse. Much, much worse," I tell myself, comparing the killer's crimes to mine.

Tomorrow is Saturday and Luke's eighteenth birthday. I've bought him a present I know he'll love and I can't wait to see his reaction. I'm taking him out to breakfast, and then we plan on going over to his house to hang out and maybe watch videos of the swimming events in the last Olympics. I'll probably stay there for lunch and we'll have the whole day together. I'll get to see his room and play with the other girl in his life – Banjo, his Beagle puppy. It's going to be heaven!

I'll meet his parents for the first time, and tell them who I am (sort of – not the whole truth, of course). I'll have to eat at the table across from them and make conversation. I'll see photographs of Andrew and maybe even his bedroom – which Luke tells me has been kept exactly as his brother left it that November morning.

It's going to be hell.

31

Damage

The door opens and we're assaulted by a baying, barking ball of fur.

"Down, Banjo. Down!" says Luke, pushing the puppy back inside the house with a foot. It immediately begins chewing on his laces.

I greet the woman who has opened the door. Luke gets his caramel hair from his mother. Her hair is thick and shoulder-length, but is somehow lifeless in a way his is not. She's an insubstantial woman – as pale as paper and almost as thin. When I shake her hand, it's limp and without pressure. Her face is bare of make-up and there are dark shadows under her eyes.

I don't know what Luke's father looks like, because he isn't there.

"He had to go in to the office. He always has to go into the office," Mrs. Naughton says, tonelessly.

She leads us, and the crazed puppy, into the living room of their small house and we sit – Luke and me on a sofa, and Luke's mother opposite us in a wingback chair. The puppy drapes itself across Luke's feet and promptly falls asleep. Mrs. Naughton fiddles with a hole in the fabric of one armrest, then picks up a glass of iced water from the coffee table between us and takes a sip, looking at me over the rim of the glass. Her gaze doesn't fix on me though, or on anything, but seems to wander around the room of its own accord. It's eleven in the morning, but the blinds on the windows are lowered two-thirds of the way.

"Luke told us about you, last night."

I am relieved; I've been stewing over it all night but I still hadn't come up with the right words to explain who I am.

"We already knew that he was dating you, of course. But last night he told us who you are. Who your mother was."

"Mrs. Naughton –"

"I found it difficult to understand why he would want to be with you, how he could stand it."

"Mom!" Luke startles the dozing puppy awake.

"But it's a funny old world and here you are, in my home," she says in that same lifeless voice. It's like she's gone, even though she's here. Even her face is blank of expression. From the way Mrs. Naughton holds the glass and takes small sips, I'm beginning to suspect the clear liquid inside is not water. From the rosy blooms in her cheeks and the unfocused stare of her gaze, I'm beginning to suspect it's not her first of the day. The fingers of her other hand stray to the hole in the armrest again and pull threads from the fabric.

"Mrs. Naughton, please, I really want you to know that I'm so sorry for the loss of Andrew. Death is always terrible, but when it's your child, and when it's caused by someone else's negligence, it must be unbearable."

"Oh it's a tragedy when your children die before you. And you're left alone."

I'm puzzled by this. Did they lose another child? Why does she think she's alone when she still has Luke, and her husband?

"He was a beautiful boy, Andrew. So bright, so good. He had such a future ahead of him. Now … it's like the lights have gone out and there's nothing left."

"But what about –" I want to point out to her that she still has Luke, that *he's* still alive, but he squeezes my hand – he's telling me not to bother.

She's not listening, anyway. She stares at the mantelpiece where there are at least ten photographs of a young man whom I presume is Andrew, and none of Luke, and then her gaze wanders back to me.

"He's gone. Gone... And you're still here."

"I'm sorry. This is too hard for you – I should never have come," I say, standing up. "Luke, this was a mistake. I think you should take me home, now."

"No," he says, taking my hand. "You're staying. We'll see you later, mom."

He leads me to his bedroom. Banjo trots ahead of us. On the way, we pass Andrew's room and I catch a brief glimpse of certificates on the wall, clothes draped over a chair, shelves jammed with books, a pair of sneakers half-tucked under the bed. There's a half-eaten chocolate bar lying on his cluttered desk; it's as if he might walk in at any moment. My stomach clenches.

"Luke, I shouldn't be here. Really. It's wrong."

But he pulls me into his room and gives me a long, steadying hug and it feels, for a moment, like everything will be all right. Then he pulls back slightly and looks at my face, the whole of it – not just parts.

"You are so beautiful," he says.

With a gentle finger, he softly traces my scar from my eye to my lip. Then he kisses it – a line of the softest touches along the length of it – and I feel completely beautiful. Luke sees me, not just my scar, and I know with a certainty born of this moment that from now on it will be just another part of me, like a tooth, or an ear. I try to put my gratitude and love into the kiss I give him. It is a long time before we break apart.

Luke's room is smaller than his brother's. The unmade bed and a narrow desk take up most of the space. On the hook behind the door hang a fistful of medals on tangled ribbons, and two pairs of goggles. A clutter of trophies congests the top of a rack of shelves mounted on the wall over the desk. The rest are strewn with piles of books, a pair of big black headphones, a collection of science-fiction DVD's and some excellent fossils – a piece of petrified wood, a fossilized fish in a square of sandstone, a delicate sand dollar, and three small ammonites.

"Snap," I say, picking up one of these and tracing its rough, ridged curves.

"I like fossils," he says. "They're proof of what happens if you stop living and adapting to change. They remind me to keep moving forward."

"So, are you ready for your present yet?" I ask eagerly.

I finger the envelope in my bag. I made a donation, on Luke's behalf, to the animal shelter – paying for the sterilization of all the animals currently in the cages, plus enough food for a month – and put the certificate they gave me in an envelope wrapped up with a wide red ribbon.

"Save it for later, I need something to look forward to if I'm going to get through lunch."

It's going to be bad, all right.

"Your mom looks like she's still really battling."

He pushes Banjo off the bed, where she has curled up on his pillow and is gnawing on what may be a pair of underpants, and flops onto the bed. I curl up next to him, my head on his shoulder. His heart thuds under my ear as he talks about his brother's life and his own grief.

"We don't have much money – you can probably see that for yourself – so that's why it was such a big thing for him to get the Harvard deal. My parents could never have afforded to send him to college otherwise."

"Are you going to be able to go?"

"I'll need to get a swimming scholarship, and I probably will – though I'm sure it won't be to some Ivy League college. It's why I'm pushing myself so hard. Well, it's part of the reason – I also like swimming."

"And you like winning."

"And I like winning," he agrees, kissing the top of my head. "Anyway, that's assuming I can get away from them." He tilts his head in the direction of his parents on the other side of the house. "My mother battles, she doesn't cope so well sometimes and needs someone to help take care of her. Dad's useless at helping her, so …"

"That leaves you?"

"That leaves me."

Then he talks about his parents, how his father has buried himself in work and his mother has "gone missing". My heart swells painfully when he says, "They've never come out and said it out loud, but I know they wish it had been me who died, not Andrew."

"Luke, how can you say that? It can't be true!"

He shrugs. "He was their favorite." There is no self-pity in his voice, just the acknowledgement of a sad truth. "Hell, he was my favorite."

And the acid of my secret eats a hole into me.

32

Choice

Lunch is an ordeal. Mr. Naughton has returned from the office, bringing take-out sandwiches with him – Mrs. Naughton doesn't look like she's up to cooking anything. We sit at the dining room table, eating the sandwiches off paper plates and drinking soda; Mrs. Naughton's "water" is nowhere to be seen. There is no cake or any reference to it being Luke's birthday. Mr. Naughton is shorter than Luke, his eyes are a more faded blue. He covers his wife's absent manner with a forced heartiness, talking non-stop about his work at a software company, and about golf and Andrew.

Interminably about Andrew.

Mrs. Naughton's dead face shows a flicker of life when her eldest son's name is mentioned and they both ramble on about his brilliance and his future and how they miss him. They don't do it to be mean to me, or to wound Luke, they just can't free themselves from their endless loop of memories and grief.

They're entitled to their pain, and I deserve to have to suck up every detail of it, but I'm getting increasingly angry on Luke's behalf. They don't tell me funny stories about when Luke was young or brag about his achievements to me. Nor do they say what a consolation he has been to them in their time of grief – and surely he must have been? They don't ask him about his life or friends or school or how his swimming is going. (They don't ask me about my life, either, but that I can understand.) In fact, they never speak directly to him at all unless they're reminding him about the time Andrew invented a solar heater ("– at the age of eleven! How do you like that, Sloane?"), or reminiscing about when he was named class valedictorian ("They gave him a standing ovation – the whole school – everyone loved our boy,") or how his girlfriend wept at his funeral ("She said she'd never find another like him!").

"And she never will," says Mrs. Naughton, with something approaching firmness. "*We* never did."

"No," says Mr. Naughton, "he's irreplaceable. But, at least we've still got –" I expect him to say "Luke" or "our other son", but instead he sighs and says, "– our memories."

"That's it," I say, placing my sandwich back onto my plate and pushing back from the table.

"You're leaving?" Mr. Naughton looks surprised.

"Yes, I'm leaving. You have a choice to make, and I'm pretty certain you don't want me around while you discuss it."

"A choice?" says Mrs. Naughton, looking at me in her vague, unfocused way.

Luke squeezes my leg in warning, but I shake my head at him – I can't stop now.

"Yes. Your loss of Andrew has been considerable, painful beyond words – I see that, I understand it. But you stand to lose even more. The way I see it, you have to choose whether you're forever going to wallow in grief and self-pity, or –"

Mrs. Naughton gasps as if I've slapped her. "How dare you?" she says shrilly. There is real conviction in her voice now.

"– or whether you're going to love the son you still have. Luke is here, right in front of you. He's alive! And he's fabulous – strong and brave and admirable. I'm sure Andrew was a fine son, but he wasn't the only one worth loving. You have a second chance here," I stand up and grip Luke's shoulder, giving him a little shake. He is staring down into his lap. His parents are gaping at me as if I'm mad. Perhaps I am. Who am I to be lecturing them?

"See *him*, celebrate *him*, love … *him!*" I end on a plea, then I place my crumpled napkin on the table and stalk to Luke's room to grab my bag.

On my way back out, the family is still sitting in stunned silence, but Luke catches up with me halfway down the front path lined with tall lavender bushes. I reach into my bag for the envelope. I want to give him his present before I go.

"You shouldn't have said that," he says.

"It's true."

"I know, but I don't think they want to hear the truth."

"Well, they *need* to hear the truth." I hear the words as I say them and my hypocrisy disgusts me.

"Perhaps. Anyway, I love you for standing up for me."

"What?" The L word. Here? Now?

He nods and grins, like he has just heard what he said and wants to confirm it.

"Yup, I lo-"

"Stop!" I yell the word. "Don't say it. Not yet. You don't know everything."

"Sloane?" He asks, puzzled.

"I said your parents need to hear the truth, but so do you ..." My voice is rising with panic.

"Are you going to lecture me too, now?"

He smiles sadly and I am pierced by the thought that this may well be the last time he ever smiles at me.

"No. I'm going to tell you the truth – the whole sad, sorry, awful truth. I should have told you ages ago."

"The truth? What do you mean?"

The smile is gone. I wish there were some way I could brace him for what's coming, but nothing I can say will change the facts.

"Luke ..." I pause, pull a head of lavender off a stalk and crumple it between my fingers; the pungent smell rises up between us. "This is what you don't know about the accident that killed Andrew. My mother *was* the one driving, and texting, and she did accidentally run a red light. But," I close my eyes, take a deep breath, force myself to meet his eyes again, "I was the one who saw those school kids. I was the one who wrenched the steering wheel to the side to miss them and sent the car into Andrew instead. It was me, not her, me."

The color drains from his face. He takes an involuntary step backwards as if reeling from a blow. His eyes go wide.

"Luke, please," I step towards him, holding out my hand. "I am so, so, sor-"

"Don't say it. Please do not say that you are sorry." His voice is cold and flat. "Like a word can make any of this better."

I nod.

"You lied. You lied to me!" he rages, his eyes now filled with contempt.

"I didn't lie, Luke, I didn't. I just assumed you knew the whole story, that the cops had told you or you'd found out at the inquest."

"I didn't go to the inquest. I didn't want to run the risk of meeting you, the girl who lived." All the old bitterness is back. "And when you discovered I didn't know? Why didn't you tell me then?"

"I tried."

"Not very hard, though, did you? When exactly did you plan to tell me – never?"

"I was scared, okay? I loved you, already then, and I couldn't face losing you."

"Well you're going to have to face it now!" He curses, curses again. "Just when I thought I could care again."

He spins on his heel and starts walking towards the house, then comes back again, smashing his hand through a lavender bush, sending the mauve florets flying.

"I thought I knew you, Sloane. I thought I could trust you. But I can't. You're a liar and I never want to see you again! I've been such a fool – I knew I should have trusted my first instincts. You've ruined my life, ruined my parents' lives, you took Andrew's."

His rage is like a hurricane coming at me full-blast, buffeting me with its force, blowing an icy chill right through the heart of me.

"Yes," I say when he stops. "All that, yes."

I look away from him at last, drop my head. It is suddenly dead-heavy, like it has picked up the weight of his pain.

I turn to go, then notice that I still have the envelope in my hands. The ribbon is half unraveled. I hand it to him.

"Here, this was for you – your birthday present. You might as well have it."

He crumples it in his fist and flings it back at me; it lands on the stone path at my feet.

"Keep it," he snarls, his face twisted into a grimace of fury. "I don't want anything from you. I don't need anything from you. Take it back – maybe you can change it, get something for yourself."

I pick up the envelope.

"Some things can't be changed, can't be taken back," I say.

Then I leave, walking all the way down the path and tossing the envelope into the trash can on the sidewalk outside Luke's house.

33

Letting go

Hold it, hold it.

I stand on the sidewalk outside Luke's house for a long while, unsure of what to do. I know only that I must hold myself together because there's something building inside of me. Something that wants out. A howl, or a scream. Perhaps it's just a whimper, but I know I can't let it out here, now. So I stand perfectly still, holding it in.

The afternoon is growing cold. A chilly, gusting breeze whips strands of hair into my face. I can't stay here. I force myself to move my hands, to find my phone and call Ed. Then I wait some more, holding on, holding in. I stare at the russet leaves scuttling down the street. A few of them bank up against my feet. It is important to keep my mind blank. If I begin to think, then I will start to feel. So I will not think about this − not here, not yet.

I hear the door of the house open behind me and a voice calls, "Hey."

I turn to see that Luke has stepped out, no further than the front step. His arms are folded across his chest.

Hold it hold it hold it.

"Do you need a lift home?" There is no softening in his face. This is mere duty and good manners.

I shake my head, wave my phone which I see is still clasped in my tight, white fingers. "Ed's coming." My voice is an unsteady croak.

He nods and goes back inside. I turn back to face the road.

I pull the threads of me in and clutch them together, holding tight, standing still as a statue in the dead leaves, waiting for my lift. Not thinking.

When Ed pulls up, I wonder if I will be able to move my feet. I feel brittle, like if I move too suddenly, I might shatter.

"The roads are nice and empty. Sure you don't want to take a shot at driving today?" he asks, as I allow myself to bend just enough to clamber into the back seat. It's warm inside the car. It smells of pizza and a love song is playing on the radio. The iciness inside my stomach roils and begins to rise.

Hold it.

"No, just straight home, please." My mouth is tight – my lips open just enough to let the words out. I keep the howl gated behind my teeth, locked up in my throat. I spend the journey staring out the window where trees shake themselves free of leaves.

"Nice to see you, stranger! Join us for supper?"

It's a smiling aunt Beryl, coming into the apartment block just as I do. She follows me through the lobby towards the elevators, clutching half a dozen grocery bags in her hands. I would offer to help her, I would, but I'm afraid that if I unclench my fingers, the threads will slip loose and what is inside will escape.

Hold it. Keep holding.

"Can I take a rain check?" I force myself to say the words.

"Sure. You've got plans?"

Oh yeah.

I nod.

Inside the elevator, I stare at the brooch on her scarf. It's a complicated art deco piece of onyx and marcasite. If I focus hard on each of the geometric facets of it, the tears dammed behind my eyes are forced to stay there.

"You okay, Sloane?" She looks at me worriedly.

"Fine. Really." The doors begin to open on my floor.

Hold it, hold it, not long now.

"How about lunch tomorrow? The triplets have learned a new song at stay-and-play and they're desperate to sing it for you. They're such sweeties, they've even memorized the actions." She starts humming the tune to "The wheels on the bus go round and round".

"Sure. Bye."

I have to force myself not to run for my apartment. My trembling fingers fumble with the keys. I can't catch my breath, something is crushing my chest from the inside.

Hold it. Hold it. Just a few seconds more.

Eventually the door is open and I'm inside and it's closed and I'm alone. I open my clenched hands, my bag falls to the floor and the threads holding me together spool loose. The shaking spreads from my hands to the rest of me. My legs can no longer hold me up. I hear paper tearing behind me as I slide down the hall wall and sit in a crumpled heap beneath the corkboard of pain.

Now.

And I let go.

It comes out as a soft mewl at first. But it grows, rapidly, to a deep sobbing which chokes my throat and hijacks my breathing. I cry. I cry for Luke. For what I've done to him and what he's done to me. For what we had and what we've lost and how we're both alone again.

And the grief expands, welling up inside of me and overflowing. There's no holding on or holding back now. I cry for Andrew, for that half-eaten bar of chocolate in that frozen room in that desolate house which is Luke's home. I cry for the absence that is where our mothers used to be. And still there is more pain inside pushing its way up and out. I cry for all the stories hanging above my head, for all the pain trapped in black ink on white paper. For the burned kid, and the alligator man and the missing girl.

And for the first time since the accident, I cry for me. For my torn face, and my struggling scrap of spleen and my stiff knee. I cry for the races I will never swim, and the dad I will never have, and the mother who will never rest her hand on my forehead. For all my scars. For all the pieces of me.

And, after an age, I'm cried out. I'm drained, hollow as an empty pool.

I pick myself up and make myself move as far as the sofa, where I can lie down and sink into blessed nothingness until tomorrow. But shimmering spots dot my sight and a jagged arc of light patterned like pieces of broken mirror begins to flicker at the side of my vision. A migraine is coming, as if to remind me that the pain is not over.

34

Breaking the silence

Luke

When I come back into the house, my parents are still sitting at the table. My mother's face is a mask of shock and outrage but, surprisingly, she's not crying. Dad's face is beet-red.

"Luke," he calls as I pass, "we need to talk to you."

"Not now," I say.

"We need –"

"NOT NOW!"

I storm to my room and slam the door behind me, then open it again and slam it again. Harder.

Sloane lied. She hid the truth from me and I was too stupid to sense that there was something off, something not quite right.

I've been burned. And I swore I never would be hurt like this again. After Andrew died, I built a thick wall between me and the rest of the world. Then she came along and scaled it, and got inside of me and I dared to care again, to trust again. And now? Now it's all ashes. Ashes and lies.

She's left her jacket behind on my bed. I snatch it up, fling it to the floor, kick it into the corner. I'm wedged in the corner, kicking and kicking and kicking when my door opens.

It's mom. "That female is standing out in front of our house. Why is she not leaving?"

I push past mom, stalk through the house, fling open the front door. She's still there, on the sidewalk, her arms clutched around her middle as if holding herself together. I call out to her and she turns around. Her face is stark white against the dark red of her hair, and pinched, like she's in pain. But I don't care. I won't care.

She says her driver is coming to fetch her. Fine. I hope he drives her off the end of the world.

Back in the house, mom and dad are waiting for me.

"I never ever want to see that person again," says mom.

This is exactly how I feel. But when she adds, "A relationship with her is not good for you," I rankle. How would she know what is or isn't good for me? She's been hands-off in the mothering department for a year, and now she suddenly wants back in? Why now – because the holy name of Andrew has been invoked?

"I'm so upset, I'm shaking," mom says, holding out a hand as evidence.

Dad puts an arm around mom's shoulders and I register that this is the first time I've seen them touching in forever.

"Now look what you've done," he says.

"Me? What have I done?"

"You've upset your mother."

"*I* didn't upset her!"

"You brought that girl into this house, knowing who she was and how it would affect us. What did you think would happen, Luke, tell us." Dad's face is growing even redder.

"What did I think would happen? I thought I would hang out with someone I liked, someone I cared about." Cared about – past tense. "Someone who understands- understood me. Someone I could talk to."

"We care about you. We understand you," says mom. "We talk."

"Oh, pul-leeze." Did I say that out loud? I've gotten used to snapping back at my parents silently in my mind.

I try to brush past them – I need the privacy of my room – but dad blocks my way.

"And just what is that supposed to mean?" he demands.

"It means ..." I pause for a fraction of a second. I have a choice here. I can be the good, understanding son and bite back the words as I usually do, or I can speak the unspeakable. My mouth decides for me. "It means that I consider this pure bullshit. It means you don't understand a thing about me, It means that you haven't cared about anything except Andrew in a year. It means that the day we lost him, I also lost my parents."

"How can you say that?" Mom looks appalled.

"And 'talk'?" I say to her. "We *never* talk! Not to each other, not about each other, not about anything that matters. We only chatter to cover the silence, because God knows what might come up, what we might have to deal with if we didn't."

Mom has a hand over her mouth, as if to press back words. Dad is swelling with rage.

"And," I continue, almost shouting at them, "please don't pretend, even to yourselves, that the reason you're upset is because you're concerned about *me*. You're only angry because Sloane dared to tell you a few home truths. She saw how things are, and she called you on it. And you don't like that, not at all. Because in this family, we don't face the truth. We hide."

Even as I say the words, I realize how crazy it is that I'm defending the person who just broke my heart. But what happened out there on the path, what she revealed – that's between us. I could throw her in the deep end of the ocean for that, but it's got nothing to do with this. With my parents. What she did in here was to hold up a mirror to our family. Or what remains of it.

"Now just you –" dad begins.

"We all hide. You hide out in your work. You," I point at my mother, "hide in your bottle and your memories. I hide out in my swimming. And that way none of us really has to face what happened. None of us has to deal with the rest of our lives. None of us actually has to *connect* with each other, or anyone else. But we're as good as dead, can't you see that?"

"You have no right to talk to us like this!" mom yells.

"You are being offensive and disrespectful," dad yells.

"Yeah, well, I'm not Andrew. He was the polite, respectful one. The perfect one." The steam is going out of me now. "But as much as you might wish it, I can't swap places with him."

I say the last words softly, almost gently. But Mom's stiff face cracks into something raw and exposed. She slaps me across the face, then bursts into tears. Dad stands frozen for a moment, then crumples into a chair, his head in his hands, his shoulders shaking.

I sigh, and turn to go to my room. But then my mother speaks, and the words pull me back.

"Luke, please – don't go. Let's talk."

35

Possible replacements

"Stop looking at him!"

"What?" I say, startled out of my daze by Sienna's irritated command.

"You were staring again. You need to stop it – have some pride, girlfriend, and stop pining over the jerk."

"Don't call him that – he's not a jerk."

"Well he's sure acting like one."

My eyes do their familiar slide to the side. Luke is sitting across the cafeteria eating his lunch, and he's not alone. It's three weeks later, and Luke has apparently moved on. With Juliet. Juliet! Jayster extraordinaire and cat-who-got-the-cream. Juliet – who smiles smugly at me to let me know it tastes delicious. He even took her to the Homecoming Dance instead of me. I spent the night babysitting the triplets and eating ice cream – flavor: pity-party. I would say I can't stand it but obviously I can, because he's been seeing her since the week after he ditched me, and I haven't dropped dead yet.

Of course, it's possible that I've turned into one of the walking dead, like L.J.'s zombies, because I don't really feel alive. I don't feel much of anything except a dull, heavy pain through the core of me. I wish mom was here to give me a hug.

"I don't get it." Sienna is talking again. "If he realized it was an accident, and was prepared to forgive your mom, then why isn't he prepared to forgive you? Okay, he might have been shocked and upset when you first told him, but after he calmed down and thought about it?"

I've wondered the same thing and I think I know why.

"I don't think it's because I was the one to pull the car to the side. I mean, it's not a fact that delighted him, but it wasn't the deal-breaker. It's that I lied to him. That's what he can't forgive."

"You never said you didn't do it."

"I never said I did, either. And he hates lying, he told me so when we were still together. I knew, after our Mexican date, that he didn't know and I didn't tell. He feels like a fool."

"He *looks* like a fool – hanging over that cow."

Sienna is nothing if not loyal, but Juliet looks nothing like a cow. She looks beautiful and happy. And unscarred. In my angry and desperate hope-fueled moments, I've wondered if Luke hooked up with her just to spite me, or to prove that I meant nothing to him, or even to distract himself – because he did it so soon. And with *her*. But seeing them now – his arm draped around her shoulders, and laughing at something she just said – I realize that's just delusional baloney. Why shouldn't he genuinely like her? (I refuse to use the other word – the L word – about them.) She's pretty and sexy and pleasant enough – to him, anyway. She's shallow enough not to come with a bunch of hectic issues. Also, there's that thing of her not having crashed a car into his brother and then lying to him about it to cover her ass.

"I hope he's happy now," Sienna says sarcastically.

"So do I," I say, but I mean it. Whatever makes him happy and gives him peace – he deserves that much. "I wish I could hate him, but I can't. I fully get it."

"Enough," says Sienna. "Time for you to move on."

"You don't understand. What we had, what I felt for him – still feel for him – you don't just *move on* from that."

"He did," she points out bluntly.

"Yeah. He did."

Juliet has her face in the crook of Luke's neck now and is nuzzling him. He must sense me, because he looks up to catch me watching him. I don't know if the pain shows in my gaze, his own is impassive. I feel myself beginning to flush and I look away.

I wish I knew what he was feeling. I've checked his profile on *Sink-or-Swim* and his Twitter stream regularly, but there are no clues there as to what's going on in his head. Or his heart.

"Sooo," says Sienna, lifting her ever-present camera to her eye and looking around at the males. "For your next BF, how about Tyrone?" She clicks off a shot.

"Get serious. He's still crushing on Juliet."

Juliet dumped Tyrone as soon as word got out that Luke had dumped me. And she came running as soon as Luke crooked his little finger. I look over to where Tyrone sits. He has his laptop open on the table in front of him but he has eyes only for Juliet. He gazes longingly at her. I follow his gaze; Juliet is now nibbling on Luke's ear. Argh!

"Tyrone looks like he still wants her and would do anything to get her back," I point out.

"Yeah, he does. And anyway, you don't want to be picking up Juliet's cast-off's." Sienna wrinkles her nose in disgust.

"I'd pick up Luke – in a heartbeat – if she cast him off."

"Something tells me that's not going to happen anytime soon."

Luke pulls his ear away from Juliet's incisors and for a minute a tiny spark of hope flickers inside me. Maybe he's getting irritated by her clinging attentions. But then I remember that he didn't like me touching his ears, either – said they were too ticklish and sensitive.

"How about L.J.?" suggests Sienna. "You seem to have a soft spot for him."

"Not to date him, Sienna. I just feel bad for him. He always seems so alone and on the outside. I can empathize. After the accident, I felt different from everyone else – separate – like I couldn't connect. People give him such a hard time, and his step-father is a real piece of work, but I don't actually much like the guy. I'm not *attracted* to him."

We speak softly, because L.J. is sitting just two tables away from us. He sits alone, taking occasional bites from the hamburger held in one hand while drawing with the other. Some fried onion and ketchup drop from the burger onto his sketch. He sticks a stubby finger into the mess and smears it around, incorporating it somehow into the drawing.

"Ew, gross," says Sienna.

She adjusts the focus on her camera and takes a few pictures. I'm looking in a different direction.

"She's feeding him now – jellybeans, I think," I say, appalled.

"Will you stop looking at him!" she snaps and reaches over to physically turn my face in the opposite direction.

"Ben," she says. "He's nice, he's single and he has no brothers – dead or alive."

"No."

She doesn't understand.

"Don't be so quick to reject him. Here, I'll take a few pictures of him for you to study in your own time."

The only pictures I study in my own time are the ones I've taken of Luke. For the first few days after our split, I poured over the pictures of him on my computer and phone, wondering and what-iffing and if-onlying. But the photos triggered the memories and the memories turned on the tear faucet. Finally, I decided that if I don't intend to spend the rest of my life ugly-crying and being disgustingly feeble, I would need to ration myself, so I'm allowed to feast my eyes for only seven minutes every night before bedtime. Being back at school, being the object of his animosity – again – was brutal. Still is.

"Sienna, you're missing the point. I'm still in love with he-who-must-not-be-looked-at. I'm not going to date anyone else. I don't *want* to date anyone else."

"Not even Coach Quinn?" she teases, taking a picture of the coach who is in the lunch line putting something on his tray. "I heard – from the horse's mouth – that the story about him and Kazinsky was bogus."

"Tempting, tempting ... but no. Not in this lifetime."

My eyes want to drift back to Luke and Juliet. Has she fed him all the jelly beans? Is he licking sugar off her fingers? I've got to stop this.

"Give me something to fix my eyes on, stat!"

"Here," says Sienna, setting her camera to display mode and shoving it into my hands.

I blink hard and try to focus all of my attention on the photographs displayed on the small screen. She's zoomed right in on her subjects and I'm amazed at the level of detail I can make out in the pictures. I can see that the items on Coach Quinn's tray are a carton of strawberry milk and an iced cupcake. I can see the freckles on Ben's blandly friendly face, and the pictures of L.J. show his sketch clearly. It's drawn in pen, with hard strokes and lines which cross and re-cross each other and have torn right through the thick paper in some places. A sun in the shape of a crying eye hovers over the portrayal of a fight between a tall human figure with a sword and a zombie. The human appears to be disemboweling the zombie, and the fried onions of L.J.'s burger trail from the creature's belly like intestines spilling into a pool of ketchup blood.

"Wow – that's pretty sick!" I say and scroll backwards through the images.

Part of me is hoping there will be ones of Luke (with Juliet out of the frame, of course), although I already know Sienna will have steered clear of photographing him out of some misplaced sense of loyalty. But there are a few of a lovesick Tyrone pining over Juliet. He looks so pathetic, it's pitiful. Struck by a sudden, horrible thought, I show Sienna the picture.

"I don't look like this, do I?'

"Are we still hot on telling the truth, or do we want a nice, white lie?" she asks.

I pull a face at her but resolve to quit sneaking peeks at Luke and to avoid looking pathetic in public. I hoist a smile onto my face. It feels unfamiliar and strange. It must look odd, too, because Sienna asks me if I'm feeling sick.

"I'm not sick. I'm just trying to look happy and well-adjusted. Though I'll settle for not looking as pathetic as Tyrone."

"Good for you," she says. Then she frowns and adds, "Keep practicing the look, though, it needs work."

In spite of myself, I smile.

"How was L.O. today, with the jer- ... with you-know-who?"

"Not too bad, I suppose."

Luckily we finished Mrs. Copeman's project while he and I were still dating, so we now have no reason to interact. I'm grateful that I chose seats far behind him in my first week of school here. They provide the perfect hiding place.

"He ignores me, and I stare at him," I tell Sienna, but one look at her face has me backing up. "Which I will stop doing, as of today. Promise! I will get my pride on and ignore him as thoroughly as he ignores me."

She nods approvingly, but it's a promise I don't get to keep, because in the very next class I share with Luke, he speaks to me.

We've just finished our English lesson with Perkel, and most of my classmates have left the room. Juliet has announced to Luke that she's off to the "little girls' room" to go reapply her eyelashes or top up her brains with toilet water, or whatever it is she and her gaggle of J-girls do in there all the time. Luke is taking his sweet time packing his things into his bag and I'm reluctant to pass by him, so I hang back, checking my phone and waiting for him to leave first. Perkel is up front doling out extra homework to L.J. who has failed to hand in the last two assignments for this class. I don't blame him. What's the point of doing any work if you know you're going to get an F?

If Perkel was picking on any other kid like this, they'd complain to their parents who would take it up with the principal. But from what I saw of L.J.'s mother and father, he won't get much help there. His mother looked too timid to say boo to a goose, and his stepfather would probably only tell him to toughen up and stop whining. I keep thinking that I should say something to somebody. I'm worried he's going to implode. I'd probably only get into trouble again if I tried to tell Perkel to ease up, but perhaps Mrs. Copeman could do something – alert the school counselor, perhaps.

L.J. wouldn't thank me for interfering, though. Maybe I should speak to him directly.

When Perkel has finished throwing his hissy fit, he walks out of the class, a self-satisfied smile on his face. L.J. lumbers back to his desk and starts shoving his things into his bag. His ears and beefy neck are flaming red.

"You okay?" I ask.

He grunts.

"Look, you could use some help."

He glares up at me and I'm taken aback by the anger on his face.

"What do you mean by that?"

I review my words, realize they could be taken to mean that I think he needs a shrink. Actually, I think he does – and I could recommend a good one – but from the look on his face, I'd better not suggest it.

"I could help you. With the homework I mean. It's not fair how he keeps loading you up with extra work."

He is still scowling at me suspiciously.

"I could do some of it for you – I've got the time now that …" I trail off, looking at Luke. His face is half-tilted towards us. Is he listening?

"I've got the time," I finish lamely.

"I don't need your help. And I don't need your pity."

"I don't pity you." I do though. I think he's wounded deeper than I am, and he could really use a friend. But I always seem to say the wrong things.

"Oh, don't you? Now that pretty boy's dumped you, you want to hook up with me – is that what you're telling me? Must be my good looks and awesome personality."

I'm sure *my* face is flaming now.

"Tell you what," says L.J., heaving his bag onto his shoulder, "why don't you come around my place tonight. I don't need your help with my English, but I could sure do with some help in extra-curricular activities. I can think of many ways for you to spend your time helping *entertain* me. It would be fu-unn."

He reaches out, trails a finger over my hand and then brushes past me before I can reply. A shudder of revulsion passes through me and I feel something close to fear. I take the pack of wipes out of my pocket, extract one and rub at my hand with it, trying to erase the feel of L.J. I look up to find Luke staring at me, quizzically.

"What?" I demand.

"Don't you think you've got enough emotional baggage to be carrying around without trying to pick up L.J.'s, too? Jeez, Sloane! Haven't you got enough pain and drama to deal with, without trying to help someone who doesn't want it?"

"I guess," is all I can find to say.

"Stay away from that guy. He's ... Just back off, okay?"

"Okay," I say. "Luke?"

"Yeah?" He stops on his way out.

"Are you ... doing okay?"

He shrugs, tilts his head in a way that could mean anything. "They told me – at the shelter – about what you did. Thanks."

It's my turn to shrug.

"Congrats on your new record," I say, desperate to prolong the conversation. "A full two seconds faster – that's impressive."

There's an awkward silence as we both look at each other. Heavy things hang in the air between us, blocking our way to each other.

"Luke –"

"Sloane –"

We both start to speak at the same moment. I wave a hand to indicate that he should go first. My breath is stuck in my throat. I can't breathe it in until I hear what he says. And I can't exhale.

"Sloane, I wanted to tell you ... I mean, I want you to know that I –"

"There you are!" Juliet appears at the doorway, wraps her painted fingernails tightly around Luke's arm and drags him out.

That you what? What do you want me to know! The words scream in my head. I actually take a few steps towards the door to go after him, to ask him to finish what he started saying but then I hear, from down the hallway, the sound of her laughter. And his.

36

Most likely to ...

I'm sitting in Art class a week later squeezing thick, wet clay and trying to force it around the wire head of my horse statue armature when Mr. Como appears at the door of the classroom. The blob of clay falls off the wire frame for the umpteenth time and I curse under my breath. I'm going to wind up submitting a little wire horsey, rather than a fabulous sculpture of same, if I can't figure out how this works. Sienna is much further along with her work. Perhaps I can pass mine off as post-modern deconstructed art – it seems to make about as much sense as some of the examples Miss Ling has shown us.

It doesn't help my concentration that half the class is buzzing with some juicy new gossip – they're bent over their phones, exclaiming and laughing. As usual, Miss Ling told us what she expects us to do, without showing us how to do it. She has spent the lesson ignoring the class while standing at the window chain-smoking cigarettes – in violation of school regulations and my respiratory health – and blowing the smoke outside. She starts and flicks the cigarette away when Como calls her name from the doorway.

"Excuse me for interrupting, but I need to speak to Sienna Southey at once," he says. He frowns and runs a finger under the collar of his shirt.

Sienna and I look at each other. She shrugs.

"I hope it's nothing bad," I say with another glance at Como, but he looks more angry than worried.

"I need to clean my hands." Sienna holds up hands covered in red clay.

"Well, be quick about it, young lady, and get yourself to my office straight away."

Sienna washes the clay off her hands at the sink in the corner of the classroom, then hurries out in the direction of the admin block. I keep expecting her to come back, and I get more and more concerned when she doesn't. I worry that something might have happened to a member of her family. I'm on my way to the cafeteria at lunch break before I see her again, rushing toward me in the crowded hall. Whatever the kids in art class were checking out on their phones, it's gone viral throughout the school. Everywhere knots of students are buzzing with excitement and laughter as they stare down at the little screens.

"Are you okay?" I ask, handing over her bag which I brought with me from Art class. "What was it? What did he want?"

Sienna looks flustered and upset.

"He wanted to chew me out!"

"What for?"

"Someone hacked into the Underground website and posted a bunch of nasty crap on there, and he thought it was me. He kept bawling me out – telling me how much I'd hurt people – and wouldn't give me a chance to explain."

"What do you mean hacked the site? What happened?"

"Someone got into my site, as an administrator or something, and posted a list, a really mean one – and it wasn't me! And Como's fuming because they also apparently hacked into the school's system and got information from private records. It took me ages to convince him that I didn't do it, and then I had to shut down the whole site before he would let me go.

"That's obviously what everyone's been looking at all morning," I say as we walk to the cafeteria. "What was on it?"

"It was one of those lists – 'Most Likely To'. You know, the student most likely to succeed, or fail, or go postal or get pregnant before twenty, that sort of thing, next to photographs of the person. And some of it is really nasty."

"Am I listed in it?" I ask, although of course I know the answer.

"... Yeah."

"What was written about me?"

"You don't want to know," says Sienna.

But I do want to know and I can find out for myself. Whoever hacked the site and posted the most-likely list must have anticipated that the site would be shut down, because they've printed off a bunch of hard copies of the list pages and left them lying on top of the steel tables in the cafeteria. Everyone descends on them and starts reading. I grab one too. I see at once that I've made the front page.

Sloane Munster: most likely to be Miss World, Tatooine. Also most likely to get plastic surgery.

"What the heck is Tatooine?" I ask Sienna.

"It's a planet in Star Wars, the one with all the mutants where Jabba the Hut lives."

"Nice," I say. "Kind."

"I'm in there, too," says Sienna pointing to an entry at the bottom of the same page.

Next to her name and picture, it says, *Most likely to: become a chimney sweep, because she's so small she can fit into chimneys and she comes with a built-in brush.*

"A built-in brush?" I ask, puzzled.

"They mean my hair," she says, pointing unconcernedly at the mop of curls which form a springy halo around her head.

She doesn't seem bothered by her entry and, to my surprise, I'm not much upset by mine either. I read through the list.

Some of it is harmless and funny, I guess. Keith, the anime cartoon artist, has been listed as *most likely to become a vampire.* Miss Ling is *most likely to win an appreciation award from the tobacco industry and least likely to win Teacher of the Year award.* But some of it, most of it, is unkind and cruel. Magda, the large girl from my Gym class, has an entry which reads: *most likely to work at MacDonald's flipping burgers and get fired for eating too many of them, before being abducted by aliens – as a food source.* Jayster Jane is: *most likely to be forgotten … wait, who were we talking about?*

The teachers haven't been spared either. Perkel is listed as being most likely to come out of the closet and be dismissed for dating one of his (male) students, Coach Quinn to join Alcoholics Anonymous (was there something in his records about a drinking problem, I wonder?), and Mrs. Copeman to win the world's worst-dresser award with a special mention of her "*ugly-ass shoes*".

"Do they know who did it?" I ask.

"No, not yet, but *I've* got a fair idea," says Sienna.

"Who?"

"I think maybe it's Tyrone."

"Tyrone Carter? Why would he do this?"

"He's a real techie. I'll bet he's up to hacking into websites and school admin systems. He may have done it to impress Juliet. You know how she always wants to know private stuff about people. And check it out – she's the only one who got something really nice written about her."

I run my fingers down the columns of names, looking for Juliet's entry, while Sienna speaks. "Maybe she asked him to do it, or maybe he was trying to get her attention."

"*Juliet Capstan*," I read, "*most likely to succeed, be prom queen, and marry a millionaire IT entrepreneur.*"

"And look what's written about Tyrone himself," Sienna says.

"*Most likely to become a self-made millionaire IT entrepreneur, and marry a beautiful prom queen,*" I read aloud. "Bit of a give-away that."

It turns out that Sienna's suspicions are correct. A minute later, Tyrone comes into the cafeteria smiling from ear to ear. A table of his friends applauds and Tyrone gives a little bow of acknowledgement. It looks like every student in the cafeteria has a copy of the list and is reading it avidly, pointing and laughing at the entries.

"For a genius, he's not too smart. He's going to be in real trouble when they put two and two together," I say. "You think he'd try to cover his tracks."

"Everyone wants some credit and acknowledgement. Everyone wants to be remembered," says the Pixie, wisely.

"What's he written about Luke?"

I'm guessing Tyrone is no fan of his rival in the Juliet stakes, and I'm right. The entry for Luke Naughton reads: "*Most likely to flub national swim trials, go prematurely bald, and have his abs turn to flab.*"

It's so ridiculous that I laugh while I look around the cafeteria for Luke. He is in his usual spot. He's also laughing, and our gazes meet for a brief moment as he crumples the paper and tosses it aside dismissively. Juliet is glowing next to him – she obviously likes the prediction about her future.

Someone who isn't laughing or glowing – unless it's with rage – is L.J. Wearing his usual red plaid shirt and big black boots, he stands in the center of the cafeteria – his face as white as his ears are red – with the paper gripped in his shaking hand. I quickly scan through the entries until I find his.

"Uh-oh," I say.

"What's it say?" asks Sienna.

"Lotus Jebediah –"

"Lotus? *Jebediah*?"

I nod. "That must be his real name."

"No wonder he would never say. I've never seen anyone who looks less like a Lotus. Or a Jebediah." Sienna, along with half the cafeteria, is staring at L.J.

"His mother looked a little out-there. Maybe she named him in a haze of hope."

"A haze of something, all right. Probably dope."

L.J.'s full entry reads: "*Lotus Jebediah: Least likely to leave a mark, except on his underpants. Also least likely to get into the Perkelator's PANTS (Perkel Appreciation 'n Thanks Society).*"

"Hey, Lotus Jebediah?" a few people call out, laughing.

I expect L.J. to shout at the hecklers, or perhaps to deck one of them, but he stays silent – rotating on the spot staring at the laughing faces around him. They're not all laughing at L.J., but I guess it feels that way to him. I don't laugh. For one thing, I don't think it's funny. For another, I'm really concerned. L.J. regularly annoys me, but I do care about him and I don't want him to harm himself. I'm considering going over to him and saying something about how everybody – almost – has had bad things said about them, how this will all blow over in a day or two, how he shouldn't let it get to him, but I remember how my previous efforts to help him have backfired. I'm still undecided about whether I should approach him when L.J. lumbers out of the room and I lose the chance.

Crunch time

Luke

I've got to talk to her. I've got to just bite the bullet and tell the truth, because I'm not being fair. Not to her and not to me, either.

It's just hard to find the right moment. And the right words.

With mom and dad, the truth just came spilling out. I was too angry to care about whether I was hurting them. And it turned out well.

But with her I need to go easy. You need to be gentle when you end someone's hope.

I'll do it today.

First instinct

For the rest of the day, the whole faculty is on the prowl in classrooms and hallways, confiscating the printed copies of the "Most Likely To" list whenever they see one. It's too little, too late. By our last lesson of the day – English with Perkel – everyone has read the list and there's a whole lot of teasing going on.

"Hey, Sloane, need the number of a plastic surgeon?" Juliet says to me as we enter Perkel's room. She is still hanging on Luke's arm.

"No thanks. Not if he's the one who worked on your face," I say.

Next to her, Luke's lip twitches, but I can't tell if it's in amusement or disapproval.

I take my usual seat up against the hallway wall, and then take up my usual slouch, face in hand, elbow on desk, eyes on the back of Luke's head, fixated on the spot where his thick, short hair twists into a pointed

V at the top of his neck. I remember touching that spot when we kissed. Then I remember my promise to Sienna and force myself to wrench my gaze away from him. I make myself stare instead at the radiator pipe which climbs up the wall beside my desk. Someone, probably Keith, has drawn a cartoon panel on the pipe and I try to make it out, but two of the picture blocks are obscured by a wad of gum.

The science students are late arriving for class. They have either spent the last hour experimenting with sulphur or eating egg-salad sandwiches, because they've brought a revolting stench into the room with them. Perkel makes a production of opening the large window beside his desk to let in the fresh air, muttering something about noxious odors which "hover through the fog and filthy air."

"And where is Mr. Hamel?" he asks the class, gesturing to L.J.'s empty seat. I realize I haven't seen L.J. since the cafeteria at lunch-time.

"I think he's, like, gone home," Juliet volunteers.

She has swapped seats with Ben and now sits in the desk just to the left of Luke from where she casts him lash-fluttering looks and endless coy smiles while she twirls her pony-tail. It's enough to make me sick and I wonder that it doesn't grate on him. Could he really have fallen for someone so different from me?

"Oh dear. Well, we shall just have to endure our disappointment and forge on without L.J.'s sparkling wit and brilliant contribution to our classwork," Perkel says snidely.

I don't laugh and neither does Luke, but we are in the minority. I wonder if Perkel can guess why L.J. is skipping, and if he has read his own entry on the list. If he has, he's not letting any reaction show.

"Please take out your copies of *Atonement*. I want us to analyze, in some detail, a passage on page 107." He parks his butt on the edge of his desk and gazes out the open window as we rifle through our books.

As he says the last words, there's a series of sounds which comes from somewhere in the school behind us. Two loud *thmps*, a pause, and then two more. And though I don't think I've ever heard them in real life before, I know exactly what they are. Gunshots.

This classroom is at the back of the school and borders the fields. The shots sounded like they came from behind us, from somewhere near the front of the school.

My head whips around. I scramble on top of my desk and stand on my toes to peer through the small, high window into the hallway. It's empty. Immediately, I look back over my shoulder at Luke. It's an automatic reflex and I can't deny the urge, no matter what I promised Sienna. His head is just turning back from the direction of the shots, turning towards Juliet.

"You okay?" he asks. Her.

"What *was* that?" she says.

"Get down. Get in there," he says and pushes her behind the desk and in the direction of the large open cabinet in which Perkel stores his books and stationery.

As I see this, as I see that Luke's first instinctive reaction is toward Juliet, even while mine is towards him, a pain shoots through my chest. I can actually feel my heart hurting, aching from this last blow. I close my eyes and breathe out slowly. It's over. Finally, I get it. I need to let go of the hope that I never knew, until this moment, I was still clinging to. It's over. If Juliet is the one he automatically checks on when there's danger, then it must be Juliet that he cares about. I have to let go of this thing. I have to find a way to disconnect from him, and from the hope that things can ever be different.

Juliet crawls into the cabinet, and tugs the door behind her. It doesn't close all the way, but she's well-hidden.

Mere seconds have passed since the shots sounded, but everything is different.

I jump in my seat when the alarm rings. It's the shrill bell used as a signal for fire or lockdown drills. But I'm guessing this isn't a drill.

39

Code Red

The alarm echoes stridently through the hallways and a voice calls, "Code red, code red!" over the intercom. It's the signal for a total lockdown, but it stuns Mr. Perkel into immobility; he simply stands and stares at us.

I get down on the floor, crouch under my desk, and look worriedly around. Everyone else is doing the same thing and speaking in urgent whispers to each other. I don't know what we're supposed to do next. There hasn't been a drill since I started at the school. I guess we just wait until we're given the all-clear. Surely Perkel should know what to do, but he's still standing frozen by the window at his desk. After a minute he pats at his pants and jacket pockets as though searching for something – the key to the classroom door?

"Mr. Perkel," I call, rising into a half-crouch and waving at him. Even I can't hear my voice above the racket. "Mr. Perkel, you need to get under the desk. It's a lockdown," I shout loudly.

He shakes himself, then goes down on his knees and lifts the tablecloth draped over his desk to crawl under it, but there's a panel fitted to the front of the desk blocking him. At that moment, the door is flung open hard. It bangs against the wall with a sharp crack and someone comes into the classroom.

It's L.J. He's wearing a camouflage-patterned hunter's vest over his plaid shirt. Pointed brass bullets are stuffed into an ammunition belt slung diagonally across his chest, one end of a pair of handcuffs dangles from a vest pocket, and he is carrying a rifle. It has a long black metal barrel and trigger, a wooden stock, and a metal bolt sticking out from the side. He kicks the door closed behind him and trains the rifle in a moving arc over the class.

There are some gasps and a few whimpers, but nobody makes a move. The girl who sits in front of me is hunched over her knees, rocking and whispering a prayer. A few desks away, Ben is crouched down low. His face is gray, and a tic twitches the corner of his eye. I'm panting as though I've just run a mile, and I feel both cold and sweaty.

"Now, L.J ..." That's Perkel talking.

I crane my neck to see him rising to stand from where he was half-hidden by the desk tablecloth. L.J. swivels to face Perkel.

"Ah, just the person I've been looking for," L.J. says. There's a deadness in his voice, but his face is alive with loathing and aggression.

Perkel takes one look at L.J.'s face and begins scrambling out of the window.

"Don't go yet – I've got something for you, Perkel!"

Moving swiftly, L.J. lifts the rifle to his shoulder, steadies the barrel against his jaw, takes aim, and pulls the trigger as Perkel launches himself through the gap. There is a deafening boom as the rifle kicks back into L.J.'s shoulder and bucks up in his hands. The shot hits the window and shatters the glass into a thousand, thousand flying fragments. I crouch over my knees on the floor, flashes of other booms and glass fragments streaking across my mind.

L.J. curses. He lumbers over to the window and peers out and down.

"Coward! Bastard zombie!" he shouts. "Look at him run, the coward."

He slides the bolt to load another round and fires off another shot. Curses, then laughs. It's a high-pitched, manic sound and it makes me want to throw up, run away screaming, curl up into a ball. Instead, I look at Luke. He's also crouched on the floor and looking at me. I don't see Juliet. She must still be hiding in the cabinet. There are screams and moans, but I can't make a sound, can't seem to breathe.

"Shut up, shut up!" shouts L.J. over the ringing alarm. "Get out of here, all of you!"

I lift my head above the top of my desk. L.J. is waving the rifle from the class to the door.

"Just get out. Go!"

Desks and chairs are knocked over as my classmates scramble for the door, pushing and shoving to get out and run for the nearest exit – via the cafeteria. I'm at the back of the throng, and Luke is not in front of me. I turn. He is standing beside his desk. A long moment hangs between us.

"Juliet," I mouth the word.

He nods – he hasn't forgotten her – and heads to the cabinet at the back of the classroom.

"Where do *you* think you're going?" L.J. asks Luke.

"I'm just –"

"Just nothing. Get out!"

Luke takes an uncertain step, but then L.J. speaks again.

"No, wait – stay where you are. I've changed my mind."

"What?" I say from where I stand, alone now, at the door. "No!"

"You still there? Well come back in, Sloane, two hostages are better than one."

"Sloane – just go. Go!" urges Luke. "L.J., let's talk."

L.J. points the rifle at Luke, who is walking toward him.

"Back up, Naughton, or you'll lose your pretty face."

Luke stops, holds his hands out from his side, palms-down. I swallow. My mouth is dry.

"Get to the back of the room, both of you," L.J. says, waving Luke and me to the back inside corner where my desk is.

We take slow, deliberate steps backwards, keeping our gaze on L.J. The alarm stops wailing and the sudden silence reverberates loudly in my ringing ears. Still pointing the weapon at us, L.J. slides the bolt at the side of the rifle back and up with a cold click. The spent cartridge flies up into the air and lands pinging on the floor, spinning on its brass end. L.J. extracts a handful of the slender bullets from the ammo belt across his hunter's vest and slides them into the chamber at the top of the rifle.

40

Priorities

Luke

I need to get her out of here. I need to keep her safe.

L.J.'s going to blow. It's coming soon, I can see it in his eyes. He's not done shooting yet, and there are only three of us left in the classroom.

Juliet's in the cupboard. If she just stays completely still and quiet, she'll be okay. Sloane and I are side-by-side in the corner, watching L.J.

He moves along the board on the front wall of the classroom to the shattered windows that look out over the fields. With his back to the wall pillar, he quickly brings his head forward and cranes around to look out of the window. At first I think he's checking to see if he can try again to get Perkel, but then I register the wail of approaching sirens and realize he's checking for cops. Of course – someone must have called the police and soon this place will be swarming with SWAT teams and expert snipers and skilled negotiators. At least, I hope it will.

Because she's got to be safe.

41

Hostage

Thank God the rest of the class got out in time. I think – I hope! – that Sienna is safe, probably still on lockdown, but I wish Luke was too. And Juliet, I guess.

Luke and I are standing beside my desk, under the poster of Byron, in the corner between the back and hallway walls. If I reach out my fingers just a few inches, I could hold his hand and I wouldn't feel so completely alone. Instead, I press my palms against my jeans.

L.J. crouches down and passes the windows quickly on his way over to where we are. He notices the door of the book cabinet is ajar and gives it a kick. There is a squeal from inside.

"Get out!"

The door doesn't move.

With the rifle still trained on Luke and me, L.J. edges the door open with a foot to reveal Juliet crouched down below the lowest shelf, sobbing noiselessly. Her face is a circle of tight, white panic. He grabs her by her ponytail and jerks her out. She falls onto her knees and he drags her along to the corner, then shoves her backwards. Luke catches her in his arms. I wrap my own around myself, as if they could protect me. The three of us huddle in the corner, facing L.J.

"So ..." L.J. pops his lips together a few times. "I missed out on my chance to rid the world of that zombie waste of space. Guess I get an F for effing revenge. At least I got Tyrone good on my way in."

"T-Tyrone?" says Juliet. "You shot him?"

"Nah. He was waiting just outside Como's office, but when he saw me coming, he ran inside and slammed the door shut behind him. Such a sack of shit!"

"We heard shots," says Luke.

"I put a couple in the office door. But I couldn't get in – it's reinforced."

L.J. tilts his head towards the shattered window, listening to the sirens. "The pigs have arrived and media should be here soon – time to make my exit and my appearance."

"This place must be surrounded by cops. If you don't surrender, you'll never get out of here alive," says Luke.

"Thanks for pointing out the obvious, teacher's pet."

The sirens are a discordant choir now; they seem to be coming from all sides of the school.

I still want to know what happened in the office.

"But you said you got Tyrone," I say.

"Damn straight! When he locked himself in Como's office, he left his things behind. But I took them out. One into his laptop," he mimes shooting downwards, "and one into his phone. You should have seen the pieces fly! Maybe I'll get another shot at him on the way out."

"Did you shoot anyone else?" Luke asks.

"Not, yet, pretty boy."

I feel a moment's relief. L.J. hasn't actually shot anyone. Yet. And surely, if he really wanted to, he could have shot any number of kids already. He's not out of control. But his next words shatter any illusion that we're not still in real danger.

"What I need is a hostage to get me out safely. And I came prepared." He pats the handcuffs protruding from his vest pocket.

"L.J., think!" Luke urges. "Where would you go? They'll get you sooner or later. Why not surrender now, before this gets any worse for you? You haven't hurt anyone yet."

"You want to be the first, pretty boy?"

Juliet starts sobbing again.

"Shut up, you," L.J. snarls at her. "It would give me great pleasure to blow off your stupid head, so don't tempt me."

Juliet's eyes bulge even further, but she silences herself with a small hiccup.

"This is Lieutenant Linda Bedley speaking." The magnified voice echoes through the halls and over the grounds. "I would like to speak to the person or persons with weapons who are inside this school. Our tactical task force has every entrance and exit to the school covered. We would like everyone to walk away from this without injury or loss of life. We need to chat about your options. Please call me on the following number." The voice recites a cell phone number.

"D-do you want to use my phone?" I ask, holding it out to L.J. in a hand which trembles.

He snatches it out of my hands and hurls it across the room. It ricochets off a window frame and flies outside.

"Chat on that, pig!" L.J. shouts after it.

Luke catches my eye, shakes his head with a miniscule movement. L.J. reaches out his beefy left hand and grabs Luke by the upper arm.

"You," he says. "Pretty Boy. You'll make a good-looking hostage."

"No!" I say, at the same time as Luke says, "It won't work."

"You know, I think it will. The cops won't kill a student with all the cameras on hand to film it. But even if they do, death by cop doesn't sound so bad to me, especially if I get the satisfaction of taking you down on my way out. That might even be a real pleasure."

I'm horrified. Paralyzed by shock and fear. *No!* is all I can think. *No, not Luke.*

"Why are you doing this, man?" says Luke. "What have you got against me? I never bullied you."

"You never *noticed* me," says L.J. "At least they saw me. Besides," he pulls Luke closer and removes the handcuffs from his vest, "you and your kind are the reason that I get given such a hard time. Everyone's supposed to look like you, act like you, swim like you. If you're gone, it'll be easier for everyone else who can't measure up."

I can't stand here, frozen like a coward, and just let this happen. I rush forward at L.J., ignore the weapon he points straight at my chest.

"No, stop! Leave him," I beg. "Don't do this."

"Back off, Sloane," Luke shouts at me. "Just back off and let him do what he must."

"Yeah – back off and leave me."

"L.J., please, you can't do this. Just give me the gun and I'll tell them it was all a mistake. I'll tell them how Perkel –"

L.J. reaches up his left hand and slams it into my shoulder, shoving me back, hard.

42

A chance

I stagger backwards from L.J.'s blow, jostle into Luke, but manage to right myself before I can fall.

"Always trying to help – like you have all the answers. You!" he barks the last word out on a bitter laugh. "As if you're any better off than me. Tell you what – you *can* finally help me now, Munster. Here," he tosses the pair of handcuffs at me, "make yourself useful and cuff Naughton to me."

He grabs Luke's right hand with his left and holds their arms extended out to me.

"Aw, we're going to make such an awesome couple, pretty boy. The TV cameras are going to get some great images. If the zombie teacher is watching, he'll get real jealous."

He urges me along, poking the rifle's barrel tip into my ribs. I am thinking quickly. I am thinking so quickly that I am sure it must show in my eyes. But I force myself to move slowly, carefully holding the handcuffs up and moving closer to their hands. There is a tiny key inserted in the cuff lock. I turn it to open the manacles.

My hands tremble as I slip one of the handcuffs over Luke's wrist, and look up into his face. He is trying to say something with his eyes, but I cannot guess what it is. Time moves slowly. I stare deeply into his wide hazel eyes as I click the handcuff closed and remove the key. My mouth is dry. I try to make more saliva.

"Sloane, I shouldn't have blamed you. I was wrong. I'm sorry I —" Luke begins, but L.J. interrupts.

"Let's make our relationship more committed. Permanent," he mocks, turning their linked hands over so that his is now on top of Luke's.

They say that in moments of extreme danger, your life flashes before your eyes. But for me, it's different. Of course it is. *His* life flashes through my mind.

I see Luke: his broad shoulders and long legs, the hair that turns the color of molasses when it's wet. I see the grace of him as he powers through the pool's water, the gentleness of his hands when he rescues a spider, the sad understanding in his eyes when he looks at his mother. I hear the laugh that transforms his face when he rolls around with his puppy, feel the touch of his finger tracing the line of my scar down my cheek, hear him telling me I'm beautiful.

He still has a chance to let go of his grief and hatred. He still has a chance for love. I have seen — can it really just have been minutes ago? — how much he cares for Juliet. He has a chance to heal his relationship with his parents, to live a full life.

I think of that shaded house where his mother sits and drinks, and of his father who keeps himself busy and talks incessantly to fill the silence. What will it do to them if they lose another son – one whom they did not appreciate while he was alive?

A world without Luke would be emptier, less than, missing some essential part.

"Hurry up," L.J. shouts at me.

I pull my gaze away from Luke's and look down to where my hands – steady now that my decision is made – cup his. I lift the other end of the handcuff and open it to its fullest extent.

Luke will be okay. A dent to his masculine pride, that's all. Maybe a little guilt. But I know better than anyone that you can live, even love, with guilt.

He'll be fine. But I'm selfish. I can't live through another loss, in a world from which he has been taken. The decision is easy really.

43

Settling debts

I move the open hand-cuff to L.J.'s hand. He lifts his wrist up to receive the restraint. Then I spin to the side, yanking Luke's manacled hand with me. In one fluid movement, I click the cuff closed over the water pipe and put the tiny key in my mouth. I swallow hard, twice, and then open my mouth wide, sticking out my tongue to show L.J. like I'm a contestant on some bug-eating reality show.

L.J.'s jaw drops. He swings the rifle around in his right hand and hits me across the face with the butt, and I crumple to the ground.

My ears are ringing and I feel dizzy. Black spots and white lights speckle my vision, and my stomach and fingers feel cold. But I will not allow myself to pass out. I stay doubled-over, hands over my face for a few seconds – long enough to spit the key I had hidden in my cheek out into my right hand. Both Luke and L.J.

are shouting at me and rattling the locked cuffs. I reach out and grab the leg of my desk with my left hand and hold onto it to steady myself, while I allow my right hand to fall down by my side, to drop the key down the side of my sneaker.

"You want me to kill you? Right now? Do you? DO YOU?" L.J. screams at me, waving the rifle in the air. "Or maybe I should kill him?" He points the rifle at Luke. "Maybe I should just blow a hole through him right now. Would you like that?"

Using the desk, I pull myself back up to my feet. I shake my head gingerly in answer to L.J.'s questions. My jaw burns like it's on fire and I can taste blood, but I feel grimly satisfied. Luke is stuck, trapped in this classroom. He won't be going anywhere with L.J. Juliet has slumped into a seat and is trembling uncontrollably. Tears stream down her face and she has a fist stuffed into her mouth to stifle her sobs.

"Get me out of here, Sloane!" Luke bellows, shocked and angry.

"I can't – I swallowed the key."

"Maybe I should just cut you open and get it out," L.J. threatens.

"L.J.," I say, stepping between him and Luke and trying to keep my voice low and calm. "You don't need him. Take me."

"No!" Luke shouts. He yanks the cuffs against the pipe.

"You can still get out of here okay, L.J. Listen." I point a finger upwards. "Can you hear? It's a chopper, probably the TV guys. You do want people to see you, don't you, to notice you? Take me. An innocent young woman always makes a better hostage. It gets the attention, makes the headlines. And the cops will be less likely to shoot if you're holding a girl."

"But you're not as pretty as he is."

"I know that!" I snap.

It's amazing, how even now, even here with a gun to my head, that still stings.

"I may not be pretty, but I am tragic-looking. I'll get the sympathy vote."

"Or maybe ..." says L.J. He is looking now at Juliet, as if considering her potential.

Oh no, you don't. I will not allow this to happen to Luke again. He will not lose another person that he cares for if I can help it. Besides, I have no great confidence in Juliet's intelligence. She's likely to do something stupid and send L.J. off the rails. But I reckon I might just be able to keep him calm. I take a step to the side to block her from L.J.'s approach.

"No, trust me, you don't want her."

"Why not? *She's* prettier than you, too."

I curse violently.

"What is it with you and *pretty*? Pretty little blonde girls are a dime a dozen. What you want is something – someone – who stands out. Someone that people will remember years from now because of how distinctive she looked. Besides, her blubbering would drive you crazy. You'd kill her just to shut her up before you even reached the main doors."

Conveniently, Juliet whimpers just then. I can tell L.J. is considering this, wavering.

The tinny, bullhorn sound of the officer's voice comes through the windows again. "This is Lieutenant Bedley of the West Lake police department. I am speaking to the person inside the building. Drop your weapons and come out the front door with your hands behind your head. If you want to speak to me directly, call me now." She repeats the telephone number.

L.J. twitches a shoulder in annoyance. His eyes flicker from the sniffling Juliet, to Luke straining against the handcuffs, to me. I force myself to step right up to L.J. We are so close that our chests are almost touching. I move in, close the distance.

"And L.J.," I say softly, looking right into his manic eyes, "you know that – with me – you can have a lot more … *fun*."

L.J. grins. Luke goes ape, wrenching and bucking against the cuffs. Blood smears his wrists where the metal cuts into his flesh.

L.J.'s smile widens. He grabs me, spins me around so that my back is pressed up against him and I'm facing Luke. While Luke pulls and jerks against the cuffs and shouts threats, L.J. strokes his free hand over my hair and then runs it down the side of my neck, and lower, over my breast.

Bile rises in my throat, but I remember Sienna talking about guilt – about settling your debts and making amends – and I swallow it down.

"This is fun and all," says L.J., "but it can wait until later. Right now, we have to go."

"No!" Luke screams. "Leave her! You can shoot these cuffs off the pipe and take me. Sloane – please!"

"Luke, shhh." I say softly, reaching out a hand to touch his wild face, lay a finger on his lips. "It's okay, really. It's better this way."

He jerks his head back, begs me, "Please don't do this. Sloane!"

"I owe you, Luke. Let me pay off my debt."

"That's crazy! There *is* no debt. There's nothing to forgive – it was an accident! I shouldn't have blamed you. The past is the past. Sloane, please – your dying won't bring back my brother!" he shouts, sagging against the cuffs.

That's when my eyes fill with tears. That's when I almost lose control. Oh, the difference those words would have made if they'd come sooner. How different everything would have been if he'd had that realization a few months, or even weeks, ago. It has come too late.

Still, the words feel like sweet forgiveness, and I take them and hold them close against my heart.

L.J. twists my arm behind my back and steers me in front of him, like a shield. He pushes me ahead of him, out of the room.

"Okay, okay, I'm moving. No need to break my arm," I tell him.

Behind me, Luke is still shouting, begging L.J. to let me go, to come back and take him instead.

"Shut up!" L.J. yells over his shoulder.

"I'll get free, L.J. I will. And if you hurt her, I'll kill you! So help me, I will."

"I said," says L.J., leaning back into the classroom and raising the rifle in one hand, "... Shut. Up."

And then he fires.

44

Frantic

"Did you shoot him? Did you shoot him?" I yell, wrenching my arm almost out of its socket as I buck back against L.J. who is pushing me in front of him down the hallway.

"Shut up!"

"Did you shoot him?" I scream, frantically struggling to get back to Luke.

"No I didn't. It was just a warning shot, Okay? Chill."

"It didn't hit him?"

"No. I probably couldn't have hit him even if I was trying. According to my stepfather, I'm useless at everything in my life and worse than useless at hitting a target – and that's when I'm shooting using two hands. So no, my shot didn't hit him." He shoves me forward a few more paces.

Please let that be true. *Please*.

"Are you telling the truth?"

"I don't lie." That's true. He tells it like it is even when it lands him in trouble.

"Do you promise, L.J.?" I twist around, trying to see his face, trying to decide if he's telling the truth.

"You're pissing me off now. Do you want me to go back and send a round through his pretty face? Because I have no problem with aim when the muzzle is actually touching the target, like it's touching you now," he says, poking me with the rifle.

"Do you promise?"

"Yes! Now shut up." He shoves me forward a few more paces and keeps pushing until I'm walking in front of him.

I think I believe him. L.J. wants to be taken seriously, but I don't think he really wants to hurt me, or anyone, come to that. I think he hates himself more than he hates anyone else. Still, he's carrying a loaded weapon. And I'm between him and the mass of armed cops outside.

He still has my arm twisted up behind my back, but he's finding it awkward to hold onto it while also keeping the end of the long barrel pressed against my side. I store this observation in my head. It might yet come in useful.

Back in the frantic chaos of the classroom, I would willingly have taken a bullet to save Luke. But now that Luke is trapped – safely, I hope – and out of danger, my mind is revving up again, trying to come up with some way to escape. Nothing brilliant occurs to me as we walk along the eerily empty hallways toward the front doors of the school. Everyone in these classrooms must be on lockdown. The doors are closed and it's quiet and still except for a strip of fluorescent lighting which buzzes and flickers overhead. I'll just have to wing it.

I'm guessing there will also be a throng of news media waiting beyond the perimeter, and I'm hoping like heck that they will make the cops more cautious, because I'm going to be in the dead center of any shootout.

L.J. must also have been expecting everyone to be waiting outside, because just as we edge around the corner that will take us into the main hall leading to the entrance, he curses in surprise and jerks us both back.

"They're already inside," L.J. says – unnecessarily, because I saw them, too. Half-a-dozen black-suited figures carrying weapons and wearing Kevlar vests, shiny black helmets, goggles and gas masks.

45

Seeing red

Luke

Sloane, my Sloane, is a hostage. I can't get my head around that. She's a hostage to a madman.

L.J. has a rifle and he's taken Sloane away. He has a rifle and he's shot with it. Shot at Perkel and Tyrone and me. What's to stop him shooting her?

I have to get to her.

I jerk and twist my hand in the cuff, try to squeeze it through the opening, but it won't come free. Maybe I could wrench the pipe loose. I yank at it as hard as I can with my other hand. But it's old plumbing, made to last, and it doesn't budge an inch.

I wish Juliet would stop sobbing and moaning so I could just think of a plan to get free.

I need something, a stick or metal bar of some kind that I could try wedge under the pipe to jimmy it away from the wall. I look around the room. There are books and folders and bags and coats that the other students left behind, but nothing that would serve as a lever.

I must get free. I've got to get to her.

"Juliet, will you please just be quiet for a few minutes. I can't think straight with you howling like that."

"But you ... you ..." she sobs, pointing a shaking finger at my chest.

I look down. And see that I am bleeding.

46

Tears

"Throw down your weapons and release your hostage!" The words are slightly muffled by the SWAT team member's gasmask, but still clearly distinguishable.

"Hey L.J., maybe –" I begin.

"I am not surrendering to those pigs!" says L.J. We're backing up through the hall, his hand clamped painfully on my shoulder, and I'm still between him and the SWAT team. "We are going to get out of this – or, at least, I am."

"Gee, thanks," I mutter.

"Shut up. Let me think."

"The back exit – at the cafeteria," I suggest.

"Do you think I'm stupid?" He shakes me so hard my teeth rattle. "They'll have both exits covered. They're probably already inside the cafeteria."

He's starting to panic. I can hear it in his voice, which has become tight and high. We come to an intersection of hallways in the center of the school, and he looks from one to another of them frantically.

"There's another exit," I say, trying to keep him calm by offering him another option. "If we can get to the gymnasium, then into the locker rooms – they have an exit to the pool. Then from the pool building, there's a door which leads directly onto the parking lot. And there's another door – an emergency exit – at the back. I think it opens out behind the pool pumps and water heaters."

Will he go for it? As he considers, my heart pounds in my chest, too big to fit beneath my ribs.

There is the sound of many feet moving in unison from somewhere behind us, then the dull thunk of something landing on the floor, followed by a soft pop. Within seconds, a cloud of white smoke is moving towards us. Suddenly, my eyes are burning and a sharp stinging in my throat makes me choke and gasp.

"Which way? Which way to the pool?" L.J. says hoarsely. He has let go of my shoulder, but the rifle is still pressed into my spine.

I walk ahead of him, moving quickly, and we disappear down the hall that leads to the gymnasium and cafeteria. I pull my t-shirt up over my nose and try to catch my breath. Tears are streaming from my burning eyes. Behind me, L.J. is coughing and cursing. The hallway stretches on endlessly, lined on either side with lockers and bulletin boards sporting posters of Thanksgiving events, football games, invitations to try out for cheerleading squads, and advertisements of items for sale. They are like the remnants of another, lost world. We pass Mrs. Copeman's room. Her door, like all the others, is closed. Have they somehow managed to evacuate, or are she and her students hidden somewhere inside?

Finally we reach the gymnasium. I push the doors open and L.J. slams them behind us, pulling the handles down to bolt them closed. My nose and throat still burn like I've swallowed fire, but I gulp down great lungful's of the clean, cool air and wipe my eyes on my sleeves.

L.J. shoves the rifle into my back.

"Quit doing that, will you?" I say.

He scowls at me, points to the locker rooms at the back of the massive space, and I move. Time is running out. In spite of what I told L.J., I'm sure that the cops will have a map of the school in their possession by now, and will have all the entrances and exits, including the emergency ones, covered. I'm not even sure that the emergency door in the pool building opens. I only ever remember seeing it closed, with a chain of some sort around its handle. If I'm going to do something, I think, as we pass the benches and lockers and showers in the boys' locker room, I'm going to have to do it soon. The beat of blood bangs in my ears, my heart hammers, my breaths are shallow. *Think!*

There might be a chance for me to make a run for it when we hit the wet area access passage. I could double-back and run into the girls' locker room.

Perhaps try to hide in a locker, or the equipment cage – under the jumble of the life-saving mannequins, buoys, kickboards and pool nets, long-handled cleaning brushes and lost property. I doubt I could make it if I tried to run back across the clear, unprotected expanse of the gym floor. I wouldn't be able to get to the doors and open them in time.

L.J. would be able to follow me and if he wanted, he'd be able to get me for sure. *Would* he follow me, though? If I were him, I'd let me go – not waste any time chasing, but just run to the exit and try to escape.

But I'm not him, and I can't be sure that he's thinking clearly or predictably. It will be a gamble, no doubt about it, but my chances aren't too great if I cooperate and go with him quietly anyway. And I'm not dying today, not if I can help it. Luke said there was nothing to forgive. I want to get back to him. I steel myself, take a deep breath.

I need to make my move … now!

47

Split second decision

L.J. must feel me tensing and bracing for the run, because he wrenches me back tight against him, crushes his big left arm around my middle.

"Don't even think about it," he warns.

He shuffles me out of the locker room, through the wet area access passage, and we emerge into the back end of the rectangular pool enclosure. It, too, is deserted. The surface of the water is mirror-smooth. The steam rising off the heated water is the only movement in the room.

"There," I point to the door, topped by a red EXIT sign, at the very back of the room, on the other side of the pool.

We lumber, like one clumsy four-footed creature, along the strip of paving between the starting blocks at the head of the pool which are to my right, and the wall of the locker rooms, to my left. If L.J. were on my right,

I could try to bump him into the pool, but he stays just to the left and behind of me. There is no way I'm strong enough to pull free from the arm clamped around my middle. Even if I could, I would be the one to fall into the pool, and he could just shoot me like a fish in a barrel.

We reach the corner of the pool and in the fraction of a second as I turn diagonally to go left to the exit, I realize he is momentarily behind me – between me and the pool. I pull forward against his arm, moving him just off-balance, and then with all my 5 foot 8 of height and weight and might, I throw myself back against him, and we both topple backwards into the pool, me on top of him.

We sink into the deep water. L.J. is pulled down by his heavy boots, thick clothes and the weight of his vest. I bring my feet up and then thrust them back down against his body, pushing him further down and giving me purchase to propel myself upwards into the air and light. I surface not far from the edge of the pool and, though my clothes make me heavy and cumbersome in the water, I make short work of swimming to the side.

Gasping and clutching the steel bar of the nearest starting block, I look around. Nothing. L.J. must still be under the water. I submerge my face and peer around down into the blue with eyes stinging from teargas and chlorine. About a dozen feet away from me, L.J. is sitting, his legs loosely crossed, on the floor of the pool. His eyes are open and he stares, unmoving, at me. A thin line of bubbles emerges from his mouth and beads upwards, like a string of pearls. The rifle has drifted away from him and lies precisely aligned, as if it had been carefully placed there, on the black strip of a lane marker.

I'm out of air. I lift my face out of the water to take a deep breath. What is he doing? What the hell is he *doing?* L.J. is making no attempt to push off from the bottom of the pool or to swim to safety. He appears to have come to a decision. I take another quick breath and look under the water. A few – a very few – tiny bubbles escape from the corner of his mouth, and then the only air bubbles are those that still cling to his hair and clothes and the hands lying loosely on his legs. His eyes close and his body tilts backwards.

I lift my head, fill my lungs with a deep breath, and dive down. What the hell am *I* doing? I have no idea. I only know that it feels like one thing to be prepared to hurt someone in the heat of the moment, and like quite another to calmly sit back and watch them drown themselves. L.J. will not be entering the "bliss of non-existence" if I can help it.

I swim down behind L.J., slip my left arm under his left armpit and across his chest, and try to tow him up. He's a dead weight and I don't budge him by much. I brace my feet against the floor of the pool and thrust up hard, pushing water down with my free hand. We start moving up. It's too slow, it's taking too long. I have no more air. I need to breathe. Now. Just when I'll have to let him go, we break the surface.

I suck in quick, loud breaths. L.J. gasps. Then he starts struggling. I thought that he had lost consciousness, but he's alert now. He fights me – pushing me off him and trying to get away. This is dangerous – we could both drown – but "Rescuing the struggling drowner" was a module covered in all three of my life-saving courses. I know what to do, and it will be an absolute pleasure to do it. I pull back my right arm and drive a fist hard and true into L.J.'s eye. He slumps back. This time he is out cold. Immediately he begins to sink again.

Pain cripples my hand and shoots up my arm. It's all I can do to hook my elbow under L.J.'s armpit and pull him into a floating position on his back, on top of me. I'm so tired, I'm ready to sink down into the water myself, but I force myself to kick my legs and to scull water with my uninjured hand. We edge slowly to the side of the pool. When we get there, I hang onto the wall. The muscles of my arms twitch and tremble, and my hand throbs painfully, but I keep it under L.J.'s arm and wedge it into the crook of his throat, keeping his head from falling forwards into the water. I can tell he's breathing, and that's a good thing, because no way would I be able to haul him out of the water. And I'm too angry to want to give him CPR.

There's a banging of doors and a stampede of feet. *Woohoo*, I think feebly, *the marines have arrived.*

"Over here," I try to shout. It comes out as more of a hoarse croak. "Help me!"

48

Victims

The paramedics have wrapped me in a crinkly foil space-blanket, with a thick woolen blanket around that. Every time I move, one or other of the blankets slips and the paramedic sitting next to me wraps me up again. He is determined that I shouldn't get cold.

L.J. has been similarly wrapped up, but he has the added accessory of white plastic strips, like computer cable ties, wrapped tightly around his wrists. And he is guarded by unsympathetic police officers, rather than a kindly paramedic.

I don't feel cold. Wet, yes, but not cold. I feel sore. The side of my face throbs where L.J. hit me with the rifle butt, and I can feel a tender, swollen lump on my jaw. My throat and eyes burn, and my hand (now buried in an ice-pack) is aching. I feel a little shaky and weak with relief and unbelievably – given the hubbub going on around me – sleepy. The surge of adrenalin which served me so well in the pool has drained from my body, leaving me feeling hollow and limp. I peer into the massive first aid box standing open next to me. There are latex gloves, face masks, saline drips, burn dressing and bandages, but nothing ... sweet. This suddenly seems like such a glaring omission that I need to tell the paramedic so.

"You guys really ought to keep donuts in your kits. And ice-cream."

"You're hungry?" he asks me.

"Kinda," I admit.

"I think I've got ..." He rummages through the pockets of his jacket, fishes out a half-empty packet of M&M's.

"Bless you," I say fervently as he hands them over. I tip the entire remainder of the packet into my mouth and bite down, cracking the hard, round balls of sweetness between my teeth. Nothing in my life has ever tasted this good, I swear it. Within minutes, I'm feeling stronger.

I stand up, and the heavy woolen blanket slides to the floor. My knees wobble for a moment, then steady. Lieutenant Bedley, who has been hovering nearby waiting to be given the all-clear by the paramedics to question me, approaches. She is shorter than me, has wispy blonde hair and a tired, severe face.

"I have some questions for you," she says.

"Yeah, but first we need to free Luke."

"Luke?"

"Yeah, Luke. He's a student here. He and Juliet are still in one of the classrooms."

"Juliet?"

"I know, right?"

"I mean, who is she – another student?"

"Oh, right. Yes. She's Luke's girlfriend – only, I'm beginning to think she isn't really. Hope has returned," I confide in her. I'm feeling a little drunk from the sugar-rush. And now that I know I'm safe, I'm feeling really anxious to see Luke.

"I wouldn't worry – it's Sloane, right? They've probably left by now. Everyone evacuated the building."

"Not so. Luke couldn't leave, he was handcuffed."

"To Juliet?"

"No, to the pipe."

"The perpetrator," she consults a small, leather-backed notebook, "L.J. Hamel, he handcuffed Luke to a pipe in a classroom?"

"No – I did that."

Lt. Bedley stands straighter, suddenly looks less tired and more severe.

"You and L.J. did this together?"

"No! *No.* He told you he took me hostage, didn't he? Look, it's a long story, and I'll be happy to give you all the details, as soon as I've freed Luke."

"You stay right where you are. I have not yet ruled you out as a potential perp. Just tell me what room these students are in and I'll send officers to check it out. We have no reports of any injuries, but I'm not taking any chances."

I'm deeply thankful no-one was hurt. Even L.J. is uninjured. I look over at him. His massive form is bent over itself, his small head in his big hands. He didn't deserve the hand life dealt him. But nor did Luke – or me, either, come to think of it. And I do think of it, standing here beside the pool, with police officers and medics milling around me.

I think of all the victims and the bullies and the pain and the death, stretching back and back. Who bullied L.J.'s stepfather, to make him so harsh? And what had been done to that person? We're all victims of victims of victims, each of us scarred by life. What makes one person swallow their pain or turn it back on themselves, and another decide to take it out on the world? It's a mystery to me. Would my mom know, if she was here to ask? Does anyone know? Luke is right about one thing – there is already too much death and pain in the world. It's time to focus on life and love.

I step around Lt. Bedley and walk away, toward the gymnasium and the hallways beyond. I'm a woman on a mission (I can almost hear Sienna humming the theme tune), and my destination is room 33. But Lt. Bedley is having none of it. She grabs me and swings me around. Her hand is hovering over the pistol holstered on her belt.

"That's it!" I say, seizing her hand and flinging it off my arm. "That's e-nough! I'm the victim here. I've been pushed, pulled and dragged through the school, shoved in the shoulder, bashed on the jaw, threatened with a rifle and half-drowned. I'm tired and sore and still hungry, dammit! Now there are still two students stuck in a classroom in this school. And I am going to free Luke – you can do what you like with Juliet. Now either shoot me where I stand – or let me go."

I guess shooting an unarmed and near-hysterical teenager is against the rules, because Lt. Bedley calls over two SWAT team members armed with automatic weapons and says to me, "You take us to this room where the two kids are, and *we'll* take it from there."

"Fine," I say. Whatever it takes to get back to Luke.

We make an odd procession. There's one storm-trooper up front, me following on like a queen, dragging my gold space-blanket like a royal train behind me, and Miss Congeniality sticking to my side like a good, suspicious cop should. The other storm-trooper brings up the rear. As we make our way through the deserted school, they check classrooms and storerooms and hallways, and keep a running commentary of our movements through their two-way radios. There is a distant metallic banging which grows louder as we walk down the hallway.

Finally, we arrive at room 33. The banging is coming from inside.

49

Drowning

"Here we are," I announce to Lt. Bedley and the armed escort.

I take a step towards the classroom door, but Lt. Bedley clamps an arm around my waist to hold me back. She pulls me to one side of the door and nods at her men.

One of them takes up position on the other side of the door, his weapon raised. The other, who I now see is carrying a heavy-looking metal battering ram, backs up a few steps and looks set to storm the door.

"Wait, wait, wait," I say.

I reach out a hand and turn the door handle.

The door swings open and the two storm-troopers charge in, shouting and aiming their weapons to the accompaniment of shrill screams from within. Ah, Juliet.

A minute later, one of the men emerges and gives Bedley the all-clear. Before she can stop me, I pull away from her, dart into the room and look into Byron's corner.

Luke is still there, hanging from the radiator pipe. His mouth is open and his eyes staring wide. My gaze fixes on his chest where a terrible blossom of blood stains his shirt. My heart stops.

"Sloane! Oh, thank God." It's Luke.

Luke is speaking. He's alive!

"He shot you?" My heart starts beating again, and anger surges up to replace panic. "He *shot* you?"

"No, he shot at the desk – I think to scare me. But a piece of wood flew up and hit me in the chest." He points to the desk beside him, where a four-inch splinter of bloodied wood lies. "It didn't go in deep, but I shouldn't have pulled it out because it's bleeding like a mother."

My eyes scan him carefully, looking for other injuries. He has Mr. Perkel's new red fire-extinguisher held clumsily in his left hand. He must have been smashing it repeatedly against the spot where the handcuffs are hooked on a pipe coupling – trying to break the cuffs or perhaps the pipe – because his manacled right hand is bleeding and swollen.

Juliet is curled up on the floor against the wall, hugging her knees and *still* sniveling. I'm amazed she hasn't dehydrated herself yet.

But Luke is alive, he's okay.

"Luke." It's all I can say. My throat is swollen closed – worse than when I was in the teargas. "Luke."

Paying no attention to the protests of the Loot and her men, I walk over to him and softly pull back his shirt to check the flesh beneath. A small hole is still trickling blood.

"Oh, Luke."

"I'm okay," he says. "Really I am. I'm just so relieved you're safe. I thought you were … But you're okay!"

"Of course I am. I'm a survivor. You know that."

I throw my arms around him and hug him – long and hard, ignoring the shooting pains this sets off in my hand, uncaring of the sudden silence from Juliet. (Now she stops crying, outrage trumping shock.)

The fire extinguisher falls to the ground with a solid clunk, and Luke's free arm embraces me tightly.

"Sloane," he whispers over and over again above my head.

When at last we break apart, my shirt is blotched red where I pressed against him. Luke looks down at me.

"Your face," he says, horrified, but he's not talking about my scar.

He softly touches the swollen side where L.J. hit me. Luke doesn't see the scar on my face; perhaps he never did. He saw the scars on the inside. We were equally damaged, me and him.

"I was a fool, Sloane. I'm sorry. I am. I was just so mad and confused. I've had my head up my ass for so long, I couldn't see clearly."

I can't say anything, but I can feel that I'm grinning like a fool. My chest feels like a tight band has fallen off it. It feels light and open, like I can breathe deeply for the first time in over a year.

The Lieutenant's men, obviously more used to action than love scenes, look to her for guidance.

"You, stand guard outside, just in case," she instructs one of them, then tells the other, "Go find some bolt-cutters or master-keys or something, so we can get the cuffs off. And bring back a paramedic – this boy needs some medical attention. Are you injured, honey?" She bends down to examine Juliet.

"I-I'm okay," says Juliet. "Do you have a Kleenex?"

I glance quickly at her. Her face is glazed with tears and, I'm delighted to see, boogers. She doesn't look nearly as pretty right now as she normally does.

The Lieutenant looks stumped for a moment, then she stoically holds out a uniformed sleeve to Juliet. After a moment's hesitation, Juliet wipes her nose on it.

I have an urge to laugh, but I guess Juliet has an urge to talk because she begins spilling her guts to Bedley, telling her everything that happened since we heard the first shot.

Luke, who has been staring only at me, staring as if he intended to memorize my features, now takes my face in his hands and bends down to kiss me. From her position on the floor behind Luke, Juliet must see this because she gasps loudly.

"Wait!" I say. "Just a sec. I need to ask you, first … what's between you and Juliet?"

Juliet sits up straight and fixes a hard gaze on Luke.

"Sloane," he says. His voice is gently chiding and he shakes his head as if at some foolishness.

"I saw you – when we heard the shots – I saw you turn from them straight to her, to check on her."

"Yeah," Juliet pipes up. "Me."

"Look, can we save this for later? I need to find out exactly what happened here, get some straight answers," says Bedley, sounding tetchy.

I ignore the interruption. I also need to find out what happened here and get some answers.

"Luke, your first instinct was to turn to her," I accuse.

"No, my first instinct, my automatic reflex, was to check on you. I was looking at you, Sloane. But you were looking out the window into the hallway – in the direction of the shots – and didn't see me."

Oh.

"But then you hid her in the closet – you made sure *she* was safe."

"There wouldn't have been enough room for both you and me, and I wanted to stick with you. I didn't want you out of my sight. Besides, I figured she wouldn't handle a crisis well, so it was better for all of us if she was out of the way."

"Well!" says Juliet angrily. She looks ready to give him a piece of her mind, but I couldn't be less interested in anything she might have to say.

"Um, can you give us a minute here," I ask the Loot.

She narrows her eyes at me and opens her mouth as if to say something sharp and official.

"You have to get all our statements. Couldn't you start with hers? Please?" I give her a pleading look.

She looks from me to Luke and back again, and something almost like a smile flickers momentarily across her severe face. Unlikely as it seems, I guess Lt. Bedley was once young and in love. She gently guides Juliet to the other side of the room and, once they sit down on a couple of chairs, Juliet begins babbling again.

I crouch down and, in front of Luke's amazed eyes, remove my sneaker and shake out the small key, holding it up for him to see.

"May I?"

"You didn't swallow it?"

"Are you kidding me? Do you know what damage something like this could do to your insides? I'd like to keep whatever organs remain, thank you very much."

I unlock the cuff from his battered wrist. The handcuffs clank back against the pipe, dangling uselessly, and Luke sags into a chair, pulling me onto his lap. I cradle his wounded hand gently in mine. I feel safe, alive, home.

I don't want to break the peace between us, but there are some things that need saying and some that need asking.

"Why did you do it, Luke? I mean, *Juliet*?" I ask him softly.

"I thought she'd piss you off the most."

I punch him – not too hard – on the shoulder at that. "She did."

"I was hurt. I felt like you could have trusted me, been honest with me."

"I should've, I know. I'm sorry, Luke. I just didn't want to ruin ... us." I motion a hand between him and me.

"It was awesome, wasn't it?"

"It was." I smile up at him, searching his eyes.

"I hurt pretty bad when it all blew to smithereens. I wanted to hate you, hated that I could only miss you. I guess I thought I could use Juliet to get over you, or at least to get back at you, but I was only kidding myself. I just wound up feeling guilty for using her. It wasn't fair. I shouldn't have hooked up with her when I didn't care for her."

I guess Juliet must have been keeping an ear on our conversation, because at that she starts bawling again, loudly.

I hear, as though from a distance, Lt. Bedley ask Juliet a question about what she thinks might have set off L.J. Good. Let her try to answer that one.

I turn in Luke's arms so that I can look directly into his eyes.

"Luke, won't it always be between us – Andrew, I mean, and the accident?"

"I guess," he says and my heart starts closing up again, tight and heavy. "We can't change what happened. But what's between us doesn't have to keep us apart. It can connect us. We're together in this. We both lost someone we love that day, and we both found someone to love afterwards."

"Andrew ..."

"Andrew was a really good guy. If he was here – and, I don't know ... sometimes I think he is – then he would tell me to stop pissing away my life and to get on with living. And with loving. And I'm sure your mom would want the same for you."

I can only nod.

"I love you, Sloane. It's that complicated, and it's that simple."

I stare up into his eyes, searching their green and golden depths. The truth is burning in them. It ignites a fire in me – a steady flame in my core that burns away my doubt.

He traces his fingers down my cheeks, over my lips. I'm aware of the fire and his touch, and also of a sudden silence from the other side of the room. Our audience must be watching again. I hear Juliet sniff indignantly and Lt. Bedley clear her throat, but I hold up a silencing hand toward them.

There's one more thing I have to say.

"And I love you, Luke."

And one more thing I have to do.

I lift my lips up to his and my fingers wrap themselves in that soft V of hair behind his neck. His arms close around me and draw me into him.

I'm done fighting. I surrender. I let go and jump off into the depths of what I can't stop and can't control. And although I'm sinking, falling into him, it's a different, a delicious kind of drowning.

And I am fully, beautifully alive.

~ the end ~

Would you like to know the inspiration behind the "Chili Queen and Chili King" scene in Scarred?

Join my Readers' Group at my website: www.joannemacgregor.com and I'll send you the exclusive, short backstory of that scene. You'll also get my newsletter once a month (at most), with advance notice of my latest releases, competitions, giveaways and offers for free review copies, as well as a behind-the-scenes peek at my writing and publication process and useful tips for new writers. I won't clutter your inbox or spam you, and I will never share your email address with anyone. Pinkie promise!

As an author, I live and die by reviews for my books. If you loved this book, please leave a review at your favorite online site. Thank you!

Feel free to connect with me via my website (www.joannemacgregor.com), Facebook, or Twitter (@JoanneMacg)!

Now available by this author: a stunning Young Adult dystopian romance, **Recoil**.

"When a skilled gamer gets recruited as a sniper in the war against a terrorist-produced pandemic, she discovers there's more than one enemy and more than one war.
The Game is real."